UNITED STATES ENCYCLOPEDIAS

THE NATIONAL PARKS ENCYCLOPEDIA

BY ALLISON LASSIEUR

Encyclopedias

An Imprint of Abdo Reference
abdobooks.com

TABLE OF CONTENTS

THE IMPORTANCE OF NATIONAL PARKS

On March 1, 1872, President Ulysses S. Grant signed the Yellowstone National Park Protection Act. This law established Yellowstone National Park in the northwestern United States. It stated that the land would be set aside as a park. For the first time, land would be federally protected for its beauty and ecological importance. Ecologically important areas are home to many plants and animals. The 1872 act recognized that Yellowstone's landscapes and wildlife needed to be preserved for future generations.

Soon, more and more national parks were created. In 1916, President Woodrow Wilson signed a law creating the National Park Service. This is a government agency that runs and maintains the country's national parks and monuments.

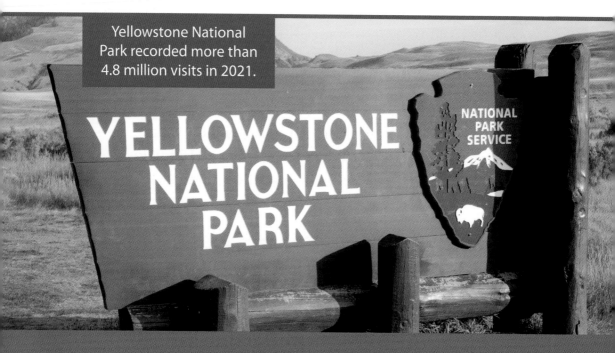

Yellowstone National Park recorded more than 4.8 million visits in 2021.

NATIONAL PARKS TODAY

National parks are important for many reasons. They preserve natural wonders, including mountains, deserts, forests, glaciers, seashores, coral reefs, islands, caves, tundra, rivers, and lakes. Animals that were once near extinction because of habitat loss and hunting

Park rangers answer questions from visitors and can tell people more about the park.

have found sanctuary in national parks. These species include bison, California condors, and black-footed ferrets. Some parks protect culturally important sites and landmarks. National parks improve mental and physical health. They are places where people can enjoy outdoor activities or rest and relax.

By 2022, the United States was home to 63 national parks. National parks remain important for conservation today. Park tourism generates billions of dollars. Over 318 million people visit US national parks every year. National parks create thousands of jobs. They are also a source of education, offering hands-on learning experiences for students. The National Park Service is dedicated to sharing the stories of the country's natural wonders with visitors of all ages.

MAP OF THE NATIONAL PARKS

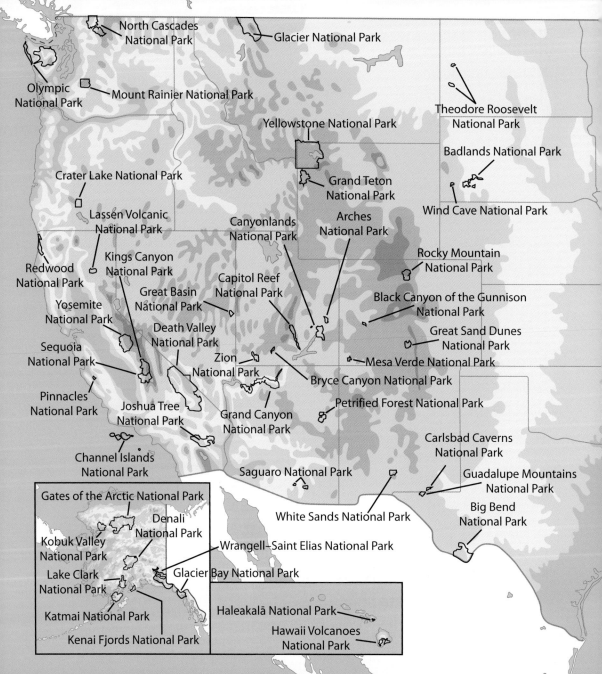

North Cascades National Park

Glacier National Park

Olympic National Park

Mount Rainier National Park

Theodore Roosevelt National Park

Yellowstone National Park

Badlands National Park

Crater Lake National Park

Grand Teton National Park

Wind Cave National Park

Lassen Volcanic National Park

Canyonlands National Park

Arches National Park

Rocky Mountain National Park

Redwood National Park

Kings Canyon National Park

Capitol Reef National Park

Black Canyon of the Gunnison National Park

Yosemite National Park

Great Basin National Park

Death Valley National Park

Great Sand Dunes National Park

Sequoia National Park

Zion National Park

Mesa Verde National Park

Bryce Canyon National Park

Pinnacles National Park

Joshua Tree National Park

Grand Canyon National Park

Petrified Forest National Park

Channel Islands National Park

Carlsbad Caverns National Park

Saguaro National Park

Guadalupe Mountains National Park

Gates of the Arctic National Park

White Sands National Park

Big Bend National Park

Denali National Park

Kobuk Valley National Park

Wrangell–Saint Elias National Park

Lake Clark National Park

Glacier Bay National Park

Katmai National Park

Haleakalā National Park

Kenai Fjords National Park

Hawaii Volcanoes National Park

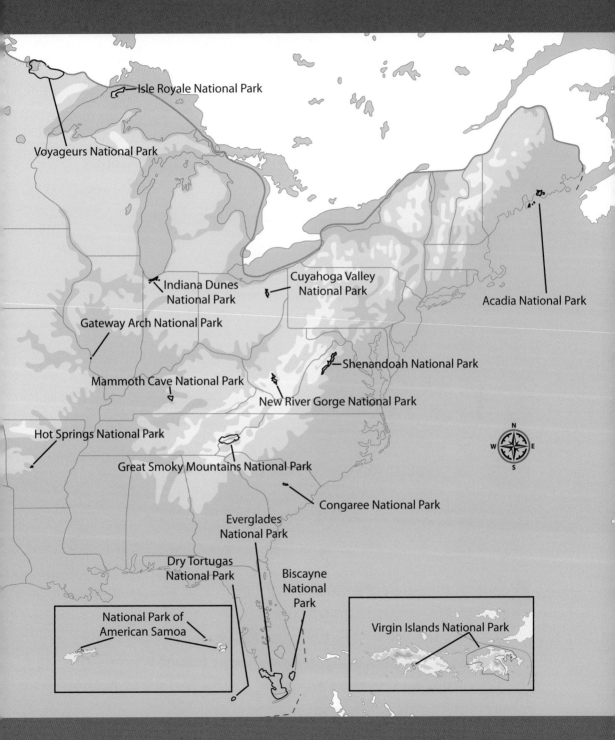

Isle Royale National Park

Voyageurs National Park

Indiana Dunes National Park

Cuyahoga Valley National Park

Acadia National Park

Gateway Arch National Park

Shenandoah National Park

Mammoth Cave National Park

New River Gorge National Park

Hot Springs National Park

Great Smoky Mountains National Park

Congaree National Park

Everglades National Park

Dry Tortugas National Park

Biscayne National Park

National Park of American Samoa

Virgin Islands National Park

ACADIA NATIONAL PARK

Location: Maine   **Established:** 1919

Forests in Acadia National Park turn magnificent colors in the fall.

Acadia National Park includes more than 73.4 square miles (190 sq km) of land along Maine's coast and islands. In 1919, it became the first national park east of the Mississippi River. Most of the park is located on Mount Desert Island—the third-largest island on the East Coast. Acadia includes beaches, mountains, forests, lakes, and wetlands.

Acadia National Park boasts the highest point along the North Atlantic coast, Cadillac Mountain. The mountain rises 1,530 feet (466 m) above sea level. From mid-October to early March, it is the first place in the continental United States where one can watch the sunrise. The mountain's altitude and eastern location make this possible.

Thunder Hole is one of the popular sites in the park. The ocean waves crash into this narrow stone inlet, causing a roar that sounds like thunder. Water may spray 40 feet (12 m) in the air as the tide hits the rocks.

Waves crash into the rocks at Thunder Hole. A walkway for a close look at the site is accessible during low tide.

HISTORY AND CULTURE

Acadia features hiking trails. It also has carriage roads that were built in the 1900s. Then, cars were not allowed on the island. Today, the carriage roads and hiking trails are still car-free. Visitors use the trails to experience Acadia's incredible beauty.

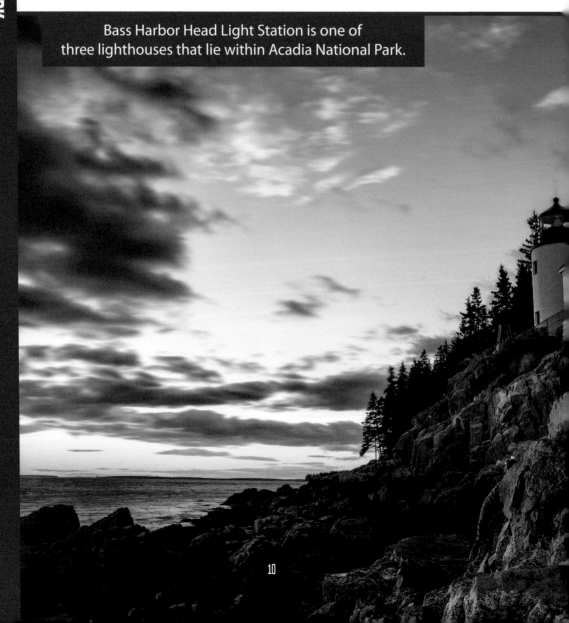

Bass Harbor Head Light Station is one of three lighthouses that lie within Acadia National Park.

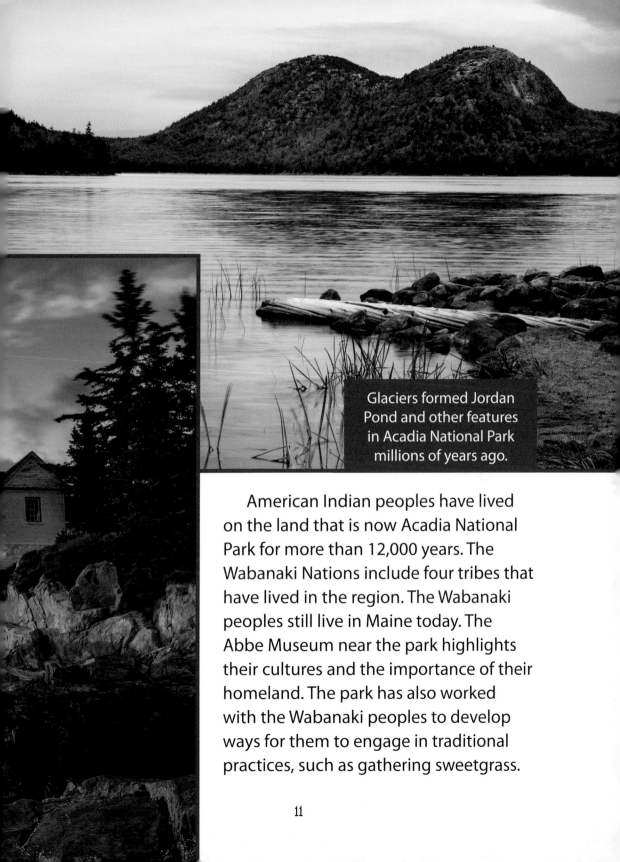

Glaciers formed Jordan Pond and other features in Acadia National Park millions of years ago.

American Indian peoples have lived on the land that is now Acadia National Park for more than 12,000 years. The Wabanaki Nations include four tribes that have lived in the region. The Wabanaki peoples still live in Maine today. The Abbe Museum near the park highlights their cultures and the importance of their homeland. The park has also worked with the Wabanaki peoples to develop ways for them to engage in traditional practices, such as gathering sweetgrass.

ARCHES NATIONAL PARK

Location: Utah   **Established:** 1971

Nearly 1.4 million people visit Arches National Park each year to see rock formations, including Delicate Arch.

Arches National Park covers 119 square miles (308 sq km) of land in southeastern Utah. The park features more than 2,000 natural red rock arches. The most famous is Delicate Arch. It has an opening that is 46 feet (14 m) tall and is the largest free-standing arch in the park. Delicate Arch appears on postage stamps and license plates in Utah.

Arches National Park is filled with sandstone canyons and rock columns, such as Park Avenue and Courthouse Towers. The Windows Section of the park is one of the most popular. It has several arches and beautiful rocky scenery. Devils Garden has narrow sandstone walls called fins, which eventually erode into arches. Rainwater has carved out these arches over time. Even today, the land at the park is constantly changing. Devils Garden also includes Landscape Arch. At 306 feet (93 m), it is the longest natural arch in North America.

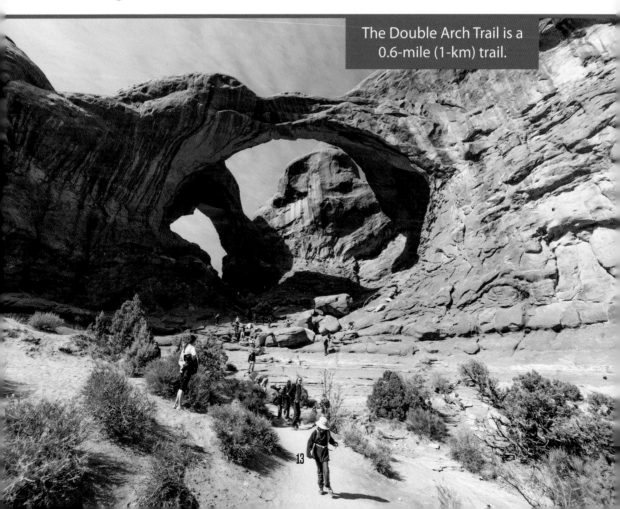

The Double Arch Trail is a 0.6-mile (1-km) trail.

Petroglyphs near the Delicate Arch were made between 1650 and 1850 CE.

THINGS TO DO

Aside from the arches, there are many other things for visitors to explore at Arches National Park. Ancient petroglyphs can be seen on the Courthouse Wash and Wolfe Ranch rock panels. These rock drawings may have been made by early ancestors of the Pueblo or Ute peoples thousands of years ago. The art depicts human figures, shields, and other symbols. The petroglyphs remain important to the Ute people today.

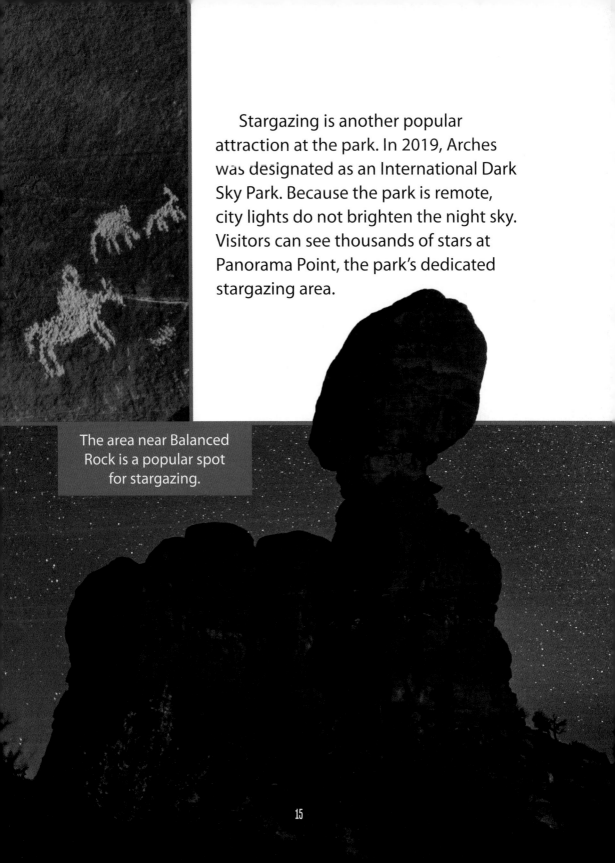

Stargazing is another popular attraction at the park. In 2019, Arches was designated as an International Dark Sky Park. Because the park is remote, city lights do not brighten the night sky. Visitors can see thousands of stars at Panorama Point, the park's dedicated stargazing area.

The area near Balanced Rock is a popular spot for stargazing.

BADLANDS NATIONAL PARK

Location: South Dakota   **Established:** 1978

Visitors can explore more than 381 square miles (987 sq km) of rock buttes, peaks, spires, and prairies at Badlands National Park. The park gets its name from the Oglala Lakota. For centuries, they called the area *mako sica*, which means "bad lands." The rough canyons and rock formations of the Badlands once made travel difficult.

Today, the Oglala Lakota and around two dozen other American Indian nations live in the Badlands. The southern section of Badlands National Park, known as the South Unit, is on tribal land. The South Unit partners with the nations located there. Together, park officials and members of these nations teach visitors about the land's importance.

The formations in Badlands National Park erode at a rate of 1 inch (2.5 cm) per year. Scientists estimate the land will erode completely in 500,000 years.

A paleontologist removes an *Archaeotherium* jaw fossil from a sample taken from Badlands National Park.

PALEONTOLOGY AND WILDLIFE

Badlands National Park is famous for its fossil beds. Paleontologists have found many kinds of fossils in the region. Fossilized seashells show that the parklands were underwater millions of years ago. Dinosaur fossils, as well as fossils of rhinoceroses, crocodiles, and camels, show how the landscape has changed over time. Badlands National Park has a strong relationship with scientists and universities studying fossils. In the summer, visitors can visit the park's Fossil Preparation Lab and watch paleontologists at work.

The park is also home to wildlife such as bighorn sheep, prairie dogs, and bison. The black-footed ferret also lives in the park. This ferret is one of the most endangered mammals in North America. Once thought to be extinct, there are now only about 120 black-footed ferrets in the Badlands.

BIG BEND NATIONAL PARK

Location: Texas   **Established:** 1935

Boquillas Canyon is the deepest canyon in Big Bend National Park, reaching a depth of 7,000 feet (2,134 m).

Big Bend National Park covers 1,252 square miles (3,243 sq km) of land along the border of Texas and Mexico. Big Bend National Park is known for its three distinct ecosystems: desert, river, and mountain. A large part of the Chihuahuan Desert lies within the park's borders. This desert is the largest one in North America. The Rio Grande flows along the border of Big Bend. The park is named for a huge bend in this river. It also includes the Chisos Mountains.

These ecosystems provide habitats for many types of wildlife, including mountain lions, bears, and bobcats. There are more types of birds and butterflies in Big Bend than in any other national park in the United States. In addition, visitors can enjoy a variety of activities. They can float down the Rio Grande, scale the Chisos Mountains, and hike in the Chihuahuan Desert.

HISTORY AND CULTURE

People have lived in the Big Bend area for thousands of years. In the Hot Springs Historic District of the park, tourists can see ancient petroglyphs on the rock walls. These drawings are thought to be between 3,000 and 8,500 years old.

The Hot Springs Historic District also includes buildings that were constructed in the early 1900s. A bathhouse was set up so people could enjoy the springs. The area quickly became a popular spot for tourists. Today, visitors can still soak in the hot springs.

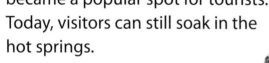

Big Bend National Park is known for its wildflowers, including bluebonnets. These flowers reach peak bloom in February and March.

BISCAYNE NATIONAL PARK

Location: Florida   **Established:** 1980

Boca Chita Key, famous for its lighthouse, is the most-visited island in Biscayne National Park.

B iscayne National Park stretches for 270 square miles (700 sq km) along the southern tip of Florida. More than 95 percent of the park is underwater. The park includes Biscayne Bay and is the largest marine park in the US National Park Service. The bay is home to many different marine creatures. The park also contains part of the last living coral reef in the continental United States.

The park includes four types of aquatic habitats: coral reefs, mangrove forests, lagoon waters, and coral limestone keys. These habitats are rich in wildlife and include manatees, manta rays, jellyfish, and sea turtles. More than 500 types of fish live in park waters. Visitors can spot birds such as loons and pelicans while on the Biscayne Birding Trail. Some visitors might even glimpse a rare Schaus swallowtail butterfly.

THINGS TO DO

Tourists enjoy many types of outdoor activities at the national park. They can canoe or kayak to mangrove forests. Snorkeling and diving are popular for underwater adventurers. Divers can investigate the remains of six shipwrecks along the park's underwater Maritime Heritage Trail.

On land, people can visit the Jones Family Historic District. This includes the house and farm of Israel Lafayette Jones, a Black farmer and entrepreneur. In the late 1800s, his family owned a pineapple farm that covered more than 0.4 square miles (1 sq km) of what is now parkland.

Green sea turtles are an endangered species that can be seen in Biscayne National Park.

Some parts of the Black Canyon receive only 33 minutes of sunlight each day.

Black Canyon of the Gunnison National Park is known for its narrow canyons and rocky cliffs. Parts of the canyon are so deep and narrow that sunlight almost never reaches the bottom. The Gunnison River formed the canyon and still flows through it today. Painted Wall, the tallest cliff in the park, stands at around 2,250 feet (686 m) high. It is also the tallest cliff in Colorado. The park covers about 48 square miles (124 sq km).

Many animal species, such as bighorn sheep, marmots, and bobcats, live in the Black Canyon. The Gunnison River is known for its trout. But other fish, such as Colorado pikeminnows and razorback suckers, also call the river home.

THINGS TO DO

Experienced hikers can tackle the challenging inner canyon. People also descend into the canyon to try their luck at wilderness fishing in the Gunnison River. The park has some of the best trout fishing in the country.

Black Canyon also allows stargazers to see a night sky free of light pollution. Light pollution happens when city light spills into the night sky and makes it harder to see the stars. Visitors can see more than 5,000 stars on clear nights at the park. The park offers astronomy programs. Each year, the park celebrates the night sky with an astronomy festival.

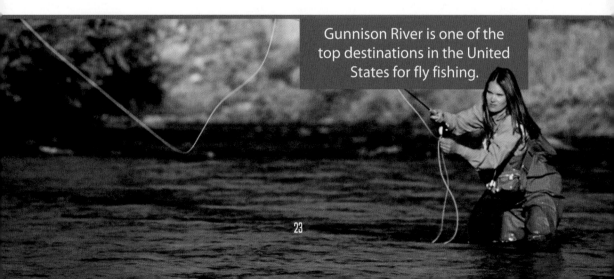

Gunnison River is one of the top destinations in the United States for fly fishing.

BRYCE CANYON NATIONAL PARK

Location: Utah   **Established:** 1928

Bryce Canyon National Park covers 56 square miles (145 sq km) and is known for its stone spires, called hoodoos. There are more hoodoos in Bryce Canyon National Park than anywhere else on Earth. More than two million visitors travel to the park each year to see these unique formations.

The hoodoos in the park formed over millions of years. Erosion causes rocks to crack. Water can get into the cracks. When the water freezes, it expands. This causes the rocks to break apart into hoodoos and other formations.

The tallest hoodoos in Bryce Canyon National Park are as tall as a ten-story building.

The Navajo Loop Trail takes hikers to lower points of Bryce Canyon.

The Bryce Amphitheater is the park's most popular attraction. It is a horseshoe-shaped area filled with colorful hoodoos. The park also has hiking trails and scenic viewpoints. Some viewpoints include Inspiration Point and Sunrise Point. People can also ride horses through parts of the canyon or spot wildlife such as falcons, elk, and prairie dogs.

Thor's Hammer, *center*, is one of Bryce Canyon's famous hoodoos.

HISTORY AND CULTURE

Paiute peoples have used Bryce Canyon and the nearby lands as a hunting and gathering area for more than 800 years. The land still holds spiritual and cultural significance to them today. The creation story about the hoodoos of Bryce Canyon is an important part of the Paiute culture. According to most versions of the story, Bryce Canyon used to be home to the *To-when-an-ung-wa*, or "Legend People." They were punished for their bad deeds by a spiritual being called Coyote. Coyote turned them into the rock hoodoos seen at the park today.

Great Basin rattlesnakes can be found in Bryce Canyon.

CANYONLANDS NATIONAL PARK

Location: Utah   **Established:** 1964

Canyonlands National Park covers more than 468 square miles (1,214 sq km) of canyons, deserts, and mesas. The rock formations of the park were carved by millions of years of erosion. Today, the park is divided into four geological districts: the Island in the Sky, the Needles, the Maze, and the Rivers. These districts are so large that it can take several days to visit all of them.

Canyonlands National Park is one of five national parks in Utah.

GEOLOGICAL DISTRICTS

Island in the Sky is a sandstone mesa standing at an elevation of 2,000 feet (610 m). Visitors can see rock layers on the canyon walls. This district also has several hiking trails, including the Shafer Trail and the Grand View Point.

The Needles district makes up the southeastern corner of the park. It is named after the many reddish-orange rock spires, or "needles," in the area. Visitors can explore the district on hiking trails or drive along a rough four-wheel-drive road.

The Maze district consists of 30 square miles (78 sq km) of canyons that twist and turn like a maze. Those who hike the challenging landscape are rewarded with stunning views of rock formations such as the Dollhouse. This is a large cluster of colorful sandstone spires.

The Rivers district includes the Green River and the Colorado River. These rivers carved into the rock layers and created the park's canyons. Many visitors also enjoy kayaking and white water rafting along the rivers.

Pictographs in Canyonlands date back to as early as 2000 BCE.

CAPITOL REEF NATIONAL PARK

Location: Utah   **Established:** 1971

Capitol Reef National Park is named for the geological formations found within its boundaries. Along with unique canyons, arches, and cliffs, the park has natural white domes made of quartz crystals. These domes look like capitol buildings. The park also has tall, rocky cliffs that were once part of an ancient underwater reef. In total, the park covers 378 square miles (979 sq km).

Many of the stone formations in Capitol Reef include fossils. The park was underwater millions of years ago. The park's

The Diné people call the Capitol Reef area the Land of the Sleeping Rainbow because of the colorful canyon walls.

Cathedral Valley and other locations in Capitol Reef offer clear views of the night sky.

Oyster Shell Reef has many fossilized oysters. Other unique formations can be seen in Cathedral Valley, which is in the northern part of the park. It has huge sandstone towers that look like cathedrals.

HISTORY AND CULTURE

More than 2,000 years ago, early Fremont and Pueblo peoples lived in the Capitol Reef area. They created pictographs that can be seen in the park today. These ancient drawings show humans, abstract designs, and animals such as sheep, deer, snakes, and dogs. Other common images include handprints. Today, many descendants of these early peoples, including the Paiute, Hopi, and Ute peoples, continue to live in the area. The park works to protect and preserve the pictographs.

CARLSBAD CAVERNS NATIONAL PARK

Location: New Mexico   **Established:** 1930

Visitors to Carlsbad Caverns National Park can go on guided tours of the King's Palace, a region within the cave system.

Carlsbad Caverns National Park stretches for 73 square miles (189 sq km) in the Chihuahuan Desert. It includes a part of this desert and more than 119 caves. The main cave is the Big Room. It is large enough to hold 14 football fields. It is the largest accessible cavern in North America.

The caves in Carlsbad Caverns National Park are made of limestone. When rainwater mixes with this rock, an acid is produced. The acid slowly eats away at the limestone. Over time, this process has created caverns and rock formations within the caves. The park is known for cave formations such as stalactites that hang from the ceilings and stalagmites that extend from the cave floors.

CAVE HISTORY

Early peoples first settled in the region near the caverns approximately 12,000 years ago. By the 1400s, the Mescalero Apache lived in the area. They called the caverns *Jadnut udebiga*, which means "home of the bat." Cave paintings and cooking pits from various peoples can be found near the cave's entrance.

In 1898, a cowhand named Jim White found the caverns while following a huge cloud of bats. He was the first person known to explore deep into the caverns. He later gave tours of the caverns and helped establish them as a national park.

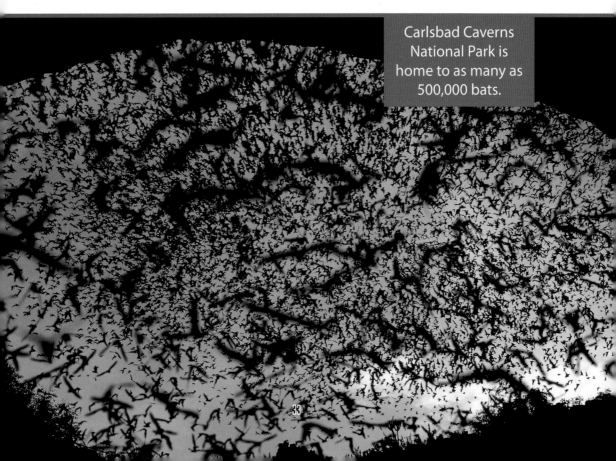

Carlsbad Caverns National Park is home to as many as 500,000 bats.

CHANNEL ISLANDS NATIONAL PARK

Location: California   **Established:** 1980

Channel Islands National Park includes five islands off the coast of southern California. They are San Miguel Island, Santa Rosa Island, Santa Cruz Island, Santa Barbara Island, and Anacapa Island. The waters surrounding these islands are also part of the park. The entire park encompasses 390 square miles (1,010 sq km). Because the park includes land and ocean, visitors can enjoy many activities. They can hike and camp. People also enjoy kayaking, diving, and snorkeling.

The Chumash people were among the earliest humans to live on the Channel Islands. They first arrived on the islands about 10,000 years ago. Today, the Chumash still live and fish in the region.

The Channel Islands are home to plants and animals that are found nowhere else on Earth.

The island fox is one of the smallest fox species in the world, but it is the largest native mammal in the park.

WILDLIFE

Many unique plants and animals can be found in the park. The Channel Islands are the only place in the world where the island fox is found. Anacapa Island has one of the largest areas of tree sunflowers. Their bright-yellow flowers bloom for only a few weeks each spring. The park's oceans are filled with sea life, such as bottlenose dolphins. Many whales, including gray whales, pass by the islands on their yearly migrations. On San Miguel Island, thousands of northern elephant seals, California sea lions, and harbor seals arrive each year to breed.

CONGAREE NATIONAL PARK
Location: South Carolina   **Established:** 2003

During the spring months, yellow butterweed flowers cover the forest floor of Congaree National Park.

Congaree National Park covers 31 square miles (81 sq km) of wilderness. It was created to protect one of the last areas of contiguous old-growth bottomland hardwood forest in North America. The hardwood forest is home to some of the tallest trees in the eastern United States. The forest canopy rises more than 100 feet (30 m) high. Congaree National Park has 15 champion trees. A champion tree is the tallest known individual of its species. The tallest tree, a loblolly pine, stands 167 feet (51 m) tall. Other champion trees in the park include sweet gum, swamp chestnut oak, laurel oak, and water hickory.

WILDLIFE AND ACTIVITIES

Congaree includes one of the most diverse ecosystems in the country. Hundreds of animal species, including river otters, bobcats, wild boar, foxes, deer, and coyote, thrive in the park. Alligators, turtles, frogs, 49 species of fish, and more than 170 species of birds can also be found in the park.

Visitors can explore the wilderness by canoeing along the 50-mile (80.5 km) Blue Trail. This water trail begins in downtown Columbia, South Carolina, and ends at the eastern edge of the park. People can explore the park by going on hikes through the forest.

Spring peepers are one of 21 known amphibian species in Congaree National Park.

CRATER LAKE NATIONAL PARK

Location: Oregon   **Established:** 1902

Crater Lake National Park is located in the Cascade mountain range and covers 286 square miles (741 sq km). The park includes Crater Lake and its islands, as well as the surrounding mountains and forests. Crater Lake formed 7,700 years ago after a volcanic eruption. The volcano collapsed, creating a large crater called a caldera. Over time, the caldera filled with rainwater and snowmelt. The region still experiences volcanic activity today.

Crater Lake gets an average of 42 feet (13 m) of snow each year.

Crater Lake is 1,943 feet (592 m) deep, making it the deepest lake in the United States. It is also the ninth-deepest lake in the world. The lake has two islands. Wizard Island was formed by cooling lava. Phantom Ship Island has tall rock formations that look like ship's sails.

Vidae Falls is a popular waterfall in Crater Lake National Park.

Visitors can hike or drive around Crater Lake's rim for spectacular views of the clear lake. Bicycling and camping are popular activities. The park is open during the winter for skiing, snowshoeing, and winter camping.

PARK HISTORY

American Indian peoples who have lived in the area have known about Crater Lake for thousands of years. Before the volcanic eruption, the Makalak people used the region for temporary camps. The Klamath are the descendants of the Makalak people. They tell stories about the eruption that have been passed down from the Makalak.

Cuyahoga Valley National Park encompasses 52 square miles (134 sq km) of land. The park was created to preserve natural areas that were threatened by land development. It includes forests, wetlands, farmlands, and a section of the Cuyahoga River. The park celebrates the people who have called this area home. This includes American Indian nations such as the Seneca and Ojibwe, as well as European and US settlers. It holds more than 250 historic structures. Visitors can ride a restored railroad and see sites along the Ohio and Erie Canal. Other park activities include hiking, biking, and kayaking.

At one time, the Cuyahoga River was one of the most polluted rivers in the country. It was so polluted that the river

Brandywine Falls is a popular waterfall in Cuyahoga Valley National Park, plunging for 60 feet (18 m).

Great blue herons are common in Cuyahoga Valley National Park. These birds are the largest herons in North America, with a wingspan of 7 feet (2 m).

caught fire in 1969. The fire pushed Ohio citizens to clean up and protect the land and the river. Today, the park continues the effort to keep the river healthy and clean.

WILDLIFE

Cuyahoga Valley National Park supports more than 40 mammal species. Coyotes, foxes, bats, bobcats, weasels, rabbits, and deer live in the forests. Beavers and muskrats can be found in the wetlands and the Cuyahoga River, along with snakes, turtles, salamanders, and frogs. The park is also home to 250 species of birds, including herons, falcons, eagles, hawks, ducks, and turkeys.

DEATH VALLEY NATIONAL PARK

Location: California and Nevada   **Established:** 1994

Zabriskie Point is a popular spot at sunrise and sunset and also offers views of Death Valley's badlands.

Death Valley National Park is the hottest place on Earth. On July 10, 1913, the park reached 134 degrees Fahrenheit (57°C), the hottest temperature ever recorded. Death Valley is also the driest national park in the United States. It typically receives less than 2 inches (5.1 cm) of rainfall each year.

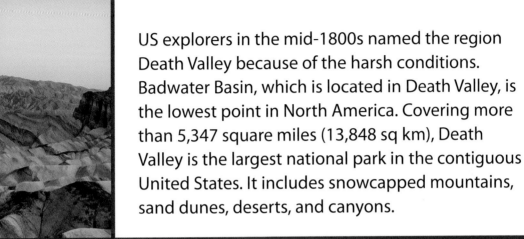

US explorers in the mid-1800s named the region Death Valley because of the harsh conditions. Badwater Basin, which is located in Death Valley, is the lowest point in North America. Covering more than 5,347 square miles (13,848 sq km), Death Valley is the largest national park in the contiguous United States. It includes snowcapped mountains, sand dunes, deserts, and canyons.

Salt flats cover Badwater Basin, which is 282 feet (86 m) below sea level.

THINGS TO DO AND WILDLIFE

The park has nearly 1,000 miles (1,610 km) of roads that allow visitors to reach popular and remote destinations in the park. Due to the extreme temperatures in the park, hiking in the valley is not recommended during the summer. Though winters are cooler, hikers should come prepared with water and other supplies. Death Valley is cooler at night, and

A kangaroo rat gets most of the water it needs from its diet of seeds, allowing it to survive in the desert.

the park offers some of the clearest views of the night sky in the world. Sunrise and sunset are also scenic times to visit the park.

More than 93 percent of the park is designated wilderness area. Visitors might spot bighorn sheep, kangaroo rats, roadrunners, and tortoises. Other desert animals such as coyotes, foxes, and jackrabbits come out at night. Mountain lions and skunks live in the mountainous areas.

Many plants grow in the desert. Wildflowers bloom in areas with more rainfall. Other desert plants have adapted to the harsh climate. For example, mesquite trees have long roots that can reach water deep underground.

Beavertail cacti are a common sight in Death Valley.

Denali National Park is the third-largest US national park. It covers more than 9,351 square miles (24,686 sq km). The park is home to Denali, the tallest mountain in North America at 20,310 feet (6,190 m). *Denali* comes from the Alaskan native language Koyukon and means "the tall one." The original purpose of the park was to protect Dall sheep. This made it the first national park created with the main purpose of protecting wildlife. Today, its goal is to preserve the pristine wildlands of Alaska and Denali.

Denali National Park is one of Alaska's eight national parks.

Male Dall sheep have large, curled horns. They live apart from female Dall sheep except during the mating season.

The park is known for its breathtaking scenery, including mountains and glaciers. Denali National Park has more than 40 named glaciers. The Kahiltna Glacier is the largest in the park, extending for about 44 miles (71 km). Most visitors travel through the park on its single 92-mile (148 km) road. They come to see the big five animals of the park: Dall sheep, grizzly bears, caribou, moose, and wolves. Hiking, biking, and camping are allowed on trails within the park. There, visitors might spot foxes and rodents, including ground squirrels, collared pika, and hoary marmots. Mountain climbers from around the world come to the park to summit Denali.

DENALI'S DOGSLED TEAM

Denali National Park is the only national park to have its own dogsled team. The first official park dogsled team arrived in the park in 1922. They patrolled the park, protecting the wildlife from poachers. The park's sled dogs have other jobs today, including transporting supplies and carrying scientists into the park's backcountry. The dogs live in kennels that are open to the public.

By the time a Denali sled dog retires, it will have traveled for 8,000 miles (12,875 km) during patrols.

Dry Tortugas National Park is one of the most remote national parks in the United States. This park lies in the Gulf of Mexico, 70 miles (113 km) west of Key West in Florida. It can only be reached by boat or seaplane. The park includes seven islands and the surrounding gulf waters and covers about 100 square miles (259 sq km).

Dry Tortugas is known for Fort Jefferson, one of the largest US forts from the 1800s. The fort is named after President Thomas Jefferson. Its purpose was to maintain control of shipping lanes in the Gulf of Mexico. Construction on the fort began in 1846, but it was never completed. It stopped in 1875

Tortugas Harbor Lighthouse sits on the walls of Fort Jefferson.

Snorkelers can see brain coral and other underwater wildlife near the walls of Fort Jefferson.

because of frequent hurricanes. Today, the fort continues to be stabilized and repaired for historic purposes.

THINGS TO DO

Much of Dry Tortugas lies underwater, where visitors can snorkel or scuba dive in the clear waters. Hundreds of shipwrecks litter the ocean's bottom. Shallow waters and heavy storms contribute to the high number of shipwrecks in the area. Divers can explore the remains of several wrecks, such as the *Avanti*, a cargo ship that sank in 1907. The park includes many coral reefs that are teeming with wildlife, such as lobsters, sea stars, sponges, and colorful reef fish. Little Africa and Texas Rock are two coral areas in the park.

EVERGLADES NATIONAL PARK
Location: Florida   **Established:** 1947

Approximately one million people visit Everglades National Park each year.

Everglades National Park is one of the most famous parks in the US National Park System. Covering 2,344 square miles (6,070 sq km) of the southern tip of Florida, the park protects the largest subtropical wilderness in North America. It contains marshlands, swamps, sloughs, and forests. It has been designated a UNESCO World Heritage site because of the wildlife it supports.

The Everglades ecosystem once covered 11,000 square miles (28,489 sq km). But in the early 1900s, settlers began draining the area to create farmlands. They did not see the ecological importance of the swamps and marshes. The drainage destroyed a large part of the Everglades. In 1947, environmentalist Marjory Stoneman Douglas wrote the best-selling book *The Everglades: River of Grass*. It showed the Everglades as a vital natural resource rather than a worthless swamp. The book helped convince people that the Everglades should become a national park to preserve what was left of this unique area.

The purple gallinule is one of many birds that live in the Everglades. It has long toes that allow it to walk across lily pads.

Many people enjoy kayaking through the waterways of the Everglades.

Visitors today can explore the park by hiking or boating. The Wilderness Waterway is a canoe trail that travels 99 miles (159 km) through the park. The park also includes several biking trails. Everglades supports more than 300 bird species and is a popular destination for bird-watching.

HABITATS AND WILDLIFE

Within the park are many different ecosystems, such as hardwood hammock forests, pinelands, coastal lowlands, and mangrove and cypress groves. These habitats support more than 1,000 plant species and more than 800 animal species. The park is home to 39 threatened and endangered animals and plants. Endangered animals include the Florida panther, West Indian manatee, and American crocodile. The Florida prairie clover is an endangered plant species with white or purple flowers.

The Everglades is home to around 200,000 alligators.

GATES OF THE ARCTIC NATIONAL PARK

Location: Alaska   **Established:** 1980

Many of the landmarks in the remote Gates of the Arctic National Park do not have official names.

Stretching across 13,238 square miles (34,286 sq km) of wilderness, Gates of the Arctic National Park is the second-largest national park in the United States. It was established to protect wild, undeveloped arctic ecosystems. The entire park is located above the Arctic Circle, and it is one of the most remote national parks. The only way to get to the park is by plane or boat. The park has no roads, trails, visitors' centers, or campgrounds. Each year, just a few thousand visitors come to the park to camp, hike, kayak, and climb the park's mountains.

Native peoples have lived in the area for more than 13,000 years. Several nations still live near the park today. The only village within park boundaries is Anaktuvuk Pass. It is home to the Nunamiut Iñupiat people. Along with the Kuuvanmiit and Koyukon peoples, the Nunamiut Iñupiat use the land for hunting, trapping, gathering, and fishing.

WILDLIFE

The park has an abundance of wildlife, including bears, wolves, lynx, beavers, musk oxen, and vast herds of caribou. Caribou herds of more than 500,000 individuals migrate through the park each year. Caribou are a vital food source for wildlife such as bears and wolves. They are also the main food source for the Nunamiut Iñupiat.

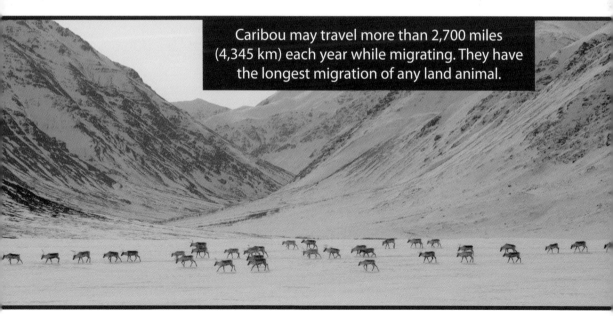

Caribou may travel more than 2,700 miles (4,345 km) each year while migrating. They have the longest migration of any land animal.

GATEWAY ARCH NATIONAL PARK

Location: Missouri   **Established:** 2018

Standing 630 feet (192 m) high and 630 feet (192 m) wide, the silver Gateway Arch is the main feature of Gateway Arch National Park. Located in Saint Louis, Missouri, the arch was completed in 1965. It was created to honor President Thomas Jefferson. In the early 1800s, Jefferson sent US explorers to map lands west of the Mississippi River. The arch sits on the banks of the Mississippi, marking the starting point of US exploration in the West. This urban park covers 0.14 square miles (0.37 sq km), making it by far the smallest national park.

Visitors to the park can ride a tram to the top of the arch and enjoy views of Saint Louis. The Gateway Arch Museum focuses on the city's history from its founding in 1764 to the construction of the Gateway Arch. The museum includes

Construction on the Gateway Arch took about 2.5 years to complete.

In 1872, Virginia Minor brought a case to the Old Courthouse. She claimed that women, as US citizens, should have the right to vote. The court ruled that citizenship did not grant voting rights.

exhibits on American Indian peoples of the area, Thomas Jefferson, the importance of the Mississippi River to Saint Louis, and the construction of the Gateway Arch.

THE OLD COURTHOUSE

The Old Courthouse is the other structure included in the national park. In 1846, Dred and Harriet Scott, two enslaved people, filed a lawsuit at the Old Courthouse. They wanted to be freed from slavery. Their case went all the way to the US Supreme Court. The Court decided the Scotts were slaves, not citizens, and did not have the right to bring a case to court. The Dred Scott case became one of the triggers of the American Civil War (1861–1865). The Old Courthouse has a museum that explains the Dred Scott case and other injustices Black people faced in Saint Louis.

GLACIER BAY NATIONAL PARK

Location: Alaska   **Established:** 1980

The Johns Hopkins Glacier in Glacier Bay National Park towers about 300 feet (91 m) above the bay.

Glacier Bay National Park is famous for its spectacular glaciers and ice-cold waters. The park includes 1,045 glaciers that cover nearly 27 percent of the park's 5,156 square miles (13,355 sq km). Glaciers move very slowly. The Johns Hopkins Glacier is the park's fastest. It can flow up to 15 feet (4.6 m) in a day. The Grand Pacific Glacier is the park's longest glacier. It blankets 40 miles (64 km) of the park with ice.

There are no roads into the park. All visitors to Glacier Bay arrive by boat or plane. Most visitors come to the park on cruise ships to see the glaciers and wildlife. Glacier Bay is home to a rich variety of land and sea life. Brown and black bears, moose, wolves, mountain goats, Sitka blacktail deer, bald eagles, porcupines, and red squirrels live in the park. Ocean mammals include harbor seals, sea otters, harbor porpoises, humpback whales, orcas, and the endangered Steller sea lion.

THE PEOPLE OF GLACIER BAY

The Huna Tlingit people have lived in the Glacier Bay region for hundreds of years. They consider the park to be their spiritual homeland. In 2016, the Huna Tlingit worked together with the National Park Service to build the Huna Ancestors' House. The Tlingit use this building for meetings, celebrations, and ceremonies. Park visitors can also come to the Ancestors' House to learn about Tlingit culture and history.

Many people come to Glacier Bay to look for whales, including humpback whales.

GLACIER NATIONAL PARK
Location: Montana   **Established:** 1910

More than 100 million tourists have visited Glacier National Park since its founding in 1910.

Glacier National Park sits on about 1,583 square miles (4,100 sq km) of mountains, lakes, and forests. The park's glaciers are more than 7,000 years old. As they melt and freeze, they reshape the landscape, carrying material from one

place to another. The park once had more than 150 active glaciers. But due to climate change, most of them have melted away. Today, there are about 26 glaciers in the park. Visitors can easily see Jackson Glacier, Salamander Glacier, Grinnell Glacier, and Sperry Glacier. Other glaciers are located deeper in the wilderness.

Blackfoot Glacier, *left*, and Jackson Glacier, *right*, are two major glaciers in Glacier National Park.

The Blackfeet Indian Reservation shares its eastern border with Glacier National Park. The nation's Lodgepole Gallery and Tipi Village allow visitors to learn more about Blackfeet culture.

For 10,000 years, people have inhabited the region where the park is located. The Blackfeet American Indian people lived in prairie areas. Other nations, including the Salish, Pend d'Oreille, and Kootenai peoples, made their homes in the forests. Today, some members of these nations live on reservations along the borders of the park. In 1982, the Native America Speaks program began in Glacier National Park. In this program, members of these different nations present stories, songs, and poetry about their peoples.

WALKING AND DRIVING

More than 700 miles (1,127 km) of hiking trails can be found in the park. Visitors can take short walks or long backcountry hikes into the park's more remote areas. One popular way to see the park is to drive along the Going-to-the-Sun Road. Travelers along this 50-mile (80 km) road see spectacular scenery, including glaciers, waterfalls, and mountains.

Experienced climbers can scale Chief Mountain.

GRAND CANYON NATIONAL PARK

Location: Arizona   **Established:** 1919

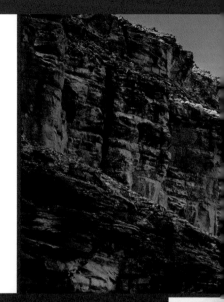

The Grand Canyon, located in Grand Canyon National Park, is considered to be one of the seven natural wonders of the world. The park covers 1,904 square miles (4,931 sq km) in northern Arizona. Stretching up to 18 miles (29 km) wide from rim to rim, the canyon is made of steep rock cliffs, ravines, and valleys. The canyon

Different minerals give the Grand Canyon its colorful, striped appearance.

People can go white water rafting on the Colorado River.

is 277 miles (446 km) long. In some places, the canyon plunges 6,000 feet (1,828 m) deep. The park is a UNESCO World Heritage site. It is also an International Dark Sky park, meaning it is an ideal place for stargazing.

Ringtails are more active at night.

The Colorado River flows through the bottom of the canyon. This river is responsible for the formation of the Grand Canyon over the past six million years. The river has eroded the dry land and carved through the rocks.

The main ecosystem of Grand Canyon National Park is semiarid desert. But within the park are diverse habitats. Forests blanket the upper elevations. Scrublands and river ecosystems thrive in lower altitudes. These areas are home to bison, elk, bighorn sheep, mule deer, mountain lions, javelinas, and ringtails. More than 450 bird species live in the park, including the Mexican spotted owl and the California condor. The condor is one of the largest and most endangered birds in North America.

A VILLAGE IN THE CANYON

Eleven American Indian nations trace their ancestries to the land where the park is located. The Havasupai still live in the area. Their home, Supai village, lies on the floor of the canyon. The residents consider themselves to be the guardians of the Grand Canyon.

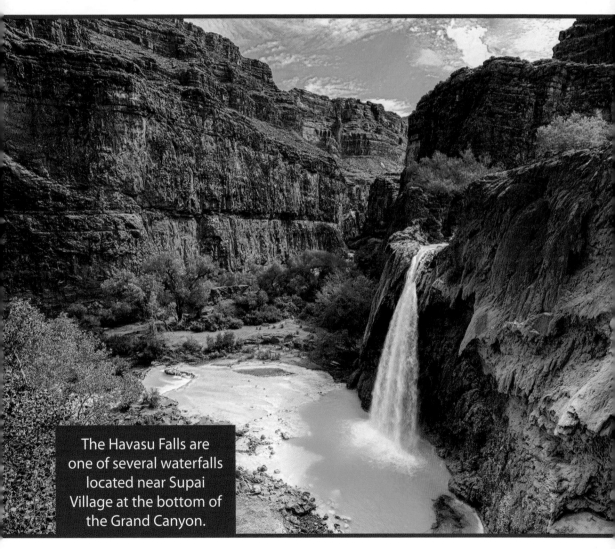

The Havasu Falls are one of several waterfalls located near Supai Village at the bottom of the Grand Canyon.

GRAND TETON NATIONAL PARK

Location: Wyoming   **Established:** 1929

Glaciers and earthquakes shaped the landscape of Grand Teton National Park.

Grand Teton National Park is one of the top ten most visited national parks. It is famous for its breathtaking scenery and more than 250 miles (402 km) of hiking trails. Located just south of Yellowstone National Park, Grand Teton covers 484 square miles (1,255 sq km). It includes the Teton Mountains, a valley called Jackson Hole, and part of the Snake River. The Tetons, popular among climbers, stretch for more than 40 miles (64 km). There are eight mountains taller than 12,000 feet (3,657 m) in this range. The tallest is Grand Teton, which rises to 13,775 feet (4,198 m). The park also includes Cascade Canyon.

When Yellowstone became a national park in 1872, people wanted to protect the Grand Tetons as well. Conservationists worried that Jackson Hole would be developed, harming the area's natural beauty. In 1927, millionaire John D. Rockefeller bought land in Jackson Hole and donated it to the government. Grand Teton National Park was created in 1929 on nearby land. And in 1950, the land Rockefeller purchased was added to the park. In recognition, the National Park Service named the road between the Grand Tetons and Yellowstone the John D. Rockefeller Parkway.

Climbing to the summit of Grand Teton typically takes six to eight hours.

THE ANIMALS OF GRAND TETON

Grizzly bears, black bears, coyotes, and wolves roam throughout Grand Teton National Park. Visitors can watch beavers, muskrats, and river otters near the pond at Schwabacher Landing and the scenic river overlook known

Wildflowers, such as Indian paintbrush, bloom in the valleys of the park in warm temperatures.

Bison eat about 24 pounds (11 kg) of plants each day.

as Oxbow Bend. Pronghorn antelope and elk live in the park too. Bison and moose graze in the meadows near the Snake River. Smaller mammals such as golden-mantled ground squirrels, marmots, and pikas are found in the boulder fields of Cascade Canyon.

Great Basin National Park covers 121 square miles (313 sq km). A basin is a landform that is lower in elevation than its surroundings. Because of this, water cannot flow out of the basin into the ocean. Instead, the water collects in lakes.

Part of the Snake mountain range is in Great Basin. Its highest peak is Wheeler Peak, which stands 13,063 feet (3,981 m) tall. It is the tallest mountain in Nevada. It is also where Wheeler Peak Glacier is located. It is the only glacier in Nevada and is made up of rocks that are frozen together.

Great Basin National Park has rare bristlecone pine trees. These trees have some of the longest life spans of any species on Earth. Prometheus was one of the oldest-known trees in

Great Basin National Park has six lakes that were formed by glaciers.

Tourists can visit the Lehman Caves only while on a ranger-led tour.

the park. It was cut down in 1964 for scientists to study. It was almost 5,000 years old. Other trees in the park may be even older.

GREAT BASIN CAVES

Great Basin National Park has more than 40 caves. A cave system called Lehman Caves contains more than 2 miles (3.2 km) of underground passageways. Between 2002 and 2015, ten new animal species were discovered in Lehman Caves. Upper Pictograph Cave is filled with ancient pictographs made by the Fremont people. They lived in the Great Basin area from 1300 to 1000 BCE. Their art depicts human figures and other images.

GREAT SAND DUNES NATIONAL PARK
Location: Colorado   **Established:** 2004

Wind continues to transform Great Sand Dunes National Park.

Great Sand Dunes National Park contains the tallest sand dunes in North America. The 233 square miles (603 sq km) of the park include a variety of ecosystems, such as forests, alpine tundra, grasslands, creeks, and wetlands. The main dune field in the park stretches for more than 30 square miles (78 sq km). Bodies of water deposit sand into the San Luis Valley, where the dunes are located. Winds blow the sand against the Sangre de Cristo Mountains. Opposing winds from the mountain range push the sand back to the valley floor, creating the dunes. The Star Dune towers more than 750 feet (229 m) high. It is the tallest dune in the park.

American Indian peoples have lived and hunted in the region for more than 11,000 years. The Ute call the sand dunes *saa waap maa nache*, which means "the sand that moves." The Ute and other nations collected bark from ponderosa pines in what is now parkland approximately 400 years ago. The bark can be used in foods and medicines.

ACTIVITIES

The most popular park activity is sand sledding or sand boarding down the dunes. Visitors can hike to the top of Star Dune, where surface temperatures of the sand can reach 150 degrees Fahrenheit (65°C). After sledding, visitors can cool off in Medano Creek, which flows along the base of the dunes.

Vendors in San Luis Valley sell and rent sand boards that allow visitors to surf down the sand dunes.

GREAT SMOKY MOUNTAINS NATIONAL PARK

Location: Tennessee and North Carolina   **Established:** 1934

Great Smoky Mountains National Park is the most visited national park in the United States. More people visit this park than Grand Canyon, Yellowstone, and Yosemite combined. The park gets its name from the smoky, blue haze that hangs over the mountains.

The vivid fall colors at Great Smoky Mountains National Park make the park a popular place to visit during that time of year.

The trail to Laurel Falls is one of the most popular hikes in Great Smoky Mountains National Park.

The park stretches for 816 square miles (2,113 sq km) and is in both Tennessee and North Carolina. It boasts some of the tallest peaks in the Appalachian Mountains, such as Mount LeConte and Clingman's Dome. Clingman's Dome has an observation tower where visitors can see as far as 100 miles (161 km) on a clear day.

People enjoy many kinds of outdoor activities in Great Smoky Mountains National Park. Cades Cove Loop Road is a popular biking trail that winds for 11 miles (18 km). Fishing is allowed year-round, and the park is known for its trout and smallmouth bass populations. Hikers can explore the park's 150 official trails for views of the forest, mountains, waterfalls, and wildlife.

The Cherokee named the Great Smoky Mountains region *Shaconage*, or "place of the blue smoke."

Black bear cubs weigh approximately 80 pounds (36 kg) by the time they are one year old.

WILDLIFE

The park is known for its abundant wildlife, such as black bears, coyotes, white-tailed deer, foxes, and bobcats. The park is also a protected area for rare animals, including the Indiana bat and the Carolina northern flying squirrel.

Guadalupe Mountains National Park covers 135 square miles (350 sq km) of rugged desert, mountains, and canyons. It has the four highest peaks in Texas. The tallest is Guadalupe Peak, at 8,751 feet (2,667 m) above sea level. Another feature of the park is El Capitan, a limestone cliff that rises more than 1,000 feet (305 m).

The Guadalupe Mountains are part of an ancient reef called Capitan Reef. Millions of years ago, this area of the United States was covered by an ocean. Today, the mountains are filled with prehistoric marine fossils. Hikers on the Permian Reef Trail can see fossils of sponges, algae, and worm-like creatures in the rocks.

The park includes many different ecosystems, including deserts, canyons, and forests. Together, they support more than

El Capitan marks the southernmost point of Guadalupe Mountains National Park.

The eastern collared lizard is one of 26 known reptile species found in Guadalupe Mountains National Park.

1,000 plant species. Some plants are not found anywhere else in the world. For instance, the Guadalupe Mountains violet is a yellow flower that grows only on the park's limestone cliffs. Animals such as mountain lions, foxes, coyotes, and bobcats live in the park. Desert areas of the park are home to rattlesnakes, lizards, scorpions, tarantulas, geckos, and desert centipedes.

THINGS TO SEE

Several historical structures highlight the park's history. One example is the Pinery, a station along the Butterfield Overland Mail route in the 1850s. The mail route consisted of approximately 200 stations. It connected Saint Louis, Missouri, to San Francisco, California. The entire journey in one direction took 25 days.

HALEAKALĀ NATIONAL PARK
Location: Hawaii   Established: 1961

Visitors to Haleakalā National Park can drive or hike to Haleakalā's summit.

Haleakalā National Park lies on Haleakalā, a dormant volcano on the island of Maui. The park covers 47 square miles (122 sq km), and more than 80 percent of the park is designated wilderness. *Haleakalā* means "house of the sun" in Hawaiian. The volcano has been a sacred area for thousands of years. People consider it the home of the gods. Hawaiian legends say Haleakalā is where the demigod Maui captured the sun and created longer days.

The volcano's peak rises more than 10,023 feet (3,055 m) above sea level. Its crater is 7.5 miles (12.1 km) long and 2.5 miles (4 km) wide. It is extremely quiet within the crater, where there is no animal life and little wind.

Haleakalā National Park is home to more endangered species than any other national park in the United States. One example is the nēnē, or Hawaiian goose. It is the state bird of Hawaii and the rarest goose in the world. The Haleakalā silversword is a plant that grows only on the crater slopes. It can live up to 100 years, but its flowers bloom only once.

THINGS TO SEE

Haleakalā National Park is divided into three areas. The Summit District has a harsh, rocky landscape where people come to see breathtaking sunrises. The Wilderness District lies in the middle of the park. Hiking trails take visitors from rocky lava fields to the ocean. The Kīpahulu District along the coast is a rich rain forest area with several scenic waterfalls.

A large banyan tree with aerial roots grows by the Pīpīwai Trail in Haleakalā National Park. The tree is more than 150 years old.

HAWAII VOLCANOES NATIONAL PARK

Location: Hawaii   **Established:** 1916

As lava cools, it forms a black rock called obsidian.

Hawaii Volcanoes National Park encompasses 524 square miles (1,357 sq km). It is located in the southeastern part of Hawaii's Big Island. It was created to protect two volcanoes, Mauna Loa and Kīlauea.

Mauna Loa means "long mountain" in Hawaiian. It is the largest active volcano on Earth. It rises 33,500 feet (10,210 m) from the seafloor to its peak. More than half of the Big Island is covered by this volcano, but only a portion of the volcano is protected by the park. Mauna Loa last erupted in 1984.

Erosion formed the
Hōlei Sea Arch from
a lava flow in Hawaii
Volcanoes National Park.

Kīlauea is smaller than Mauna Loa, rising 4,009 feet (1,222 m) above sea level. It is one of the most active volcanoes in the world. *Kīlauea* means "spewing." The volcano has been erupting regularly since 1983. It is famous for a molten lava lake inside its Halemaumau caldera. Native Hawaiians believe that Kīlauea is the home of Pele, the Hawaiian goddess of fire and creation.

THINGS TO SEE

Park visitors can hike the Crater Rim Trail that runs along Kīlauea's summit. More experienced backpackers can hike up to the top of Mauna Loa. The Halemaumau Trail leads through a rain forest. People may see hāpuu, a type of tree fern,

Kīlauea erupted in 1983, sending a fountain of lava 164 feet (50 m) in the air.

on their hikes. These ferns grow near the
summit of Kīlauea and can reach 35 feet
(10.7 m). Hikers can also take trails to see
petroglyphs that were created by
Native Hawaiian people. Two
scenic roadways, Crater
Rim Drive and Chain of
Craters Road, offer
spectacular views of
the volcanoes and
volcanic formations.

HOT SPRINGS NATIONAL PARK
Location: Arkansas   **Established:** 1921

By the time spring water reaches the base of the Hot Water Cascade in Hot Springs National Park, the water has cooled down enough to touch.

Hot Springs National Park covers 8.7 square miles (22.5 sq km) of downtown Hot Springs, Arkansas, as well as many nature trails outside the town. The park lies in the Ouachita Mountains, which stretch through Arkansas and Oklahoma. The 10-mile (16-km) Sunset Trail in the park offers scenic mountain views.

The town and park sit on top of fault lines, cracks that run deep under Earth's surface. Land near fault lines can move around. This led to the creation of the hot springs. Rainwater can fall deep into the faults. It is very hot deep underground, and the water heats up. As the land around the fault shifts, hot water is brought up to the surface. The water that reaches the surface is about 140 degrees Fahrenheit (60°C). The park has 17 hot springs that produce about 700,000 gallons (3.2 million L) of water each day. The park has drinking fountains that allow people to safely drink water from the hot springs.

PARK HISTORY

Early US settlers believed the hot water had healing properties. In 1832, the US Congress reserved the area to protect the springs, making Hot Springs the oldest government-protected park. In the 1880s, many elegant bathhouses were built on a street now called Bathhouse Row. When the National Park Service was created in 1916, it gained control of the Hot Springs reserve. Hot Springs became an official national park in 1921.

The Ozark Bathhouse was built in 1922 with influences from Spanish architecture.

INDIANA DUNES NATIONAL PARK

Location: Indiana   **Established:** 2019

Indiana Dunes National Park covers 23.4 square miles (60.7 sq km) and includes 15 miles (24 km) of shoreline along Lake Michigan. The park's inland sand dunes rise 200 feet (60 m) above the beaches. The dunes are made when waves from the lake wash sand onto shore. Wind blows the sand inland, where it piles into dunes. Beach grass along the shoreline holds the sand dunes in place. Over time, small dunes joined together to create the huge dunes of the park. The landscape is constantly changing. The Mount Baldy dune is one of the tallest dunes in the park. It moves 5 to 10 feet (1.5 to 3 m) a year. It has buried whole trees in sand.

Grasses and plants grow on some sand dunes in Indiana Dunes National Park. Their roots prevent the sand from blowing away.

Many people enjoy sunbathing and water activities on the beaches in Indiana Dunes.

Indiana Dunes was created to protect the area's forests, wetlands, rivers, and prairies. The park's endangered black oak savannah is one of the last remaining oak savannahs in the United States. Oak savannahs are areas where grasslands and oak trees grow together. The park also protects endangered species such as the Karner blue butterfly and the Pitcher's thistle plant.

THINGS TO DO

Visitors to Indiana Dunes enjoy many types of outdoor activities. They can swim and fish in Lake Michigan. They can camp within the park. Indiana Dunes has many hiking and biking trails. During the winter, people can cross-country ski and snowshoe in the park.

ISLE ROYALE NATIONAL PARK
Location: Michigan   **Established:** 1940

Rock Harbor Lighthouse is the oldest lighthouse in Isle Royale National Park.

Isle Royale is a remote park located in northwestern Lake Superior. It includes the lake's largest island, Isle Royale, along with more than 450 smaller islands. The park encompasses 850 square miles (2,201 sq km) of land and water. The only way to reach Isle Royale National Park is by boat or seaplane.

The Ojibwe people have historically used the islands for fishing, hunting, and trapping. They call Isle Royale *Minong*, "the good place." Today, the Grand Portage Band of the Ojibwe continue to fish and gather plants in the park. They also conduct ceremonies and celebrations on Isle Royale.

Thousands of years ago, early peoples used copper from the island to make weapons and ornaments. Today, park visitors can still see the ancient copper mines. The island is also one of only two places where the Michigan state gem, Isle Royale greenstone, can be found.

WILDLIFE

Isle Royale is home to about 20 mammal species. These include the gray wolf. The first island wolves walked over the frozen lake from Canada in 1948. The Isle Royale wolf population dropped sharply in 2012. Wolves are an important indicator of ecosystem health. Scientists are working to introduce more wolves to the park.

The surrounding waters provide habitat for more than 60 types of fish. Common fish include the northern pike, yellow perch, and lake whitefish. The rare coaster brook trout is only found in Lake Superior and can be seen in Isle Royale.

Scientists monitor the populations of wolves and moose at Isle Royale National Park as part of an ongoing study of predator-prey relationships.

JOSHUA TREE NATIONAL PARK

Location: California   **Established:** 1994

Joshua trees typically do not grow more than 40 feet (12 m) tall.

Joshua Tree National Park covers 1,242 square miles (3,217 sq km). It lies at the intersection of the Mojave and Colorado Deserts. The park was created to protect desert plants and wildlife, including the Joshua trees for which the park is named. Joshua trees live only in the Mojave portion of the park. Despite their name, these tall plants are not trees. They are succulents, which have fleshy tissue to store water. Joshua trees grow to about 40 feet (12 m) tall. Joshua trees can live for more than 150 years.

Visitors to the park enjoy climbing the huge piles of granite boulders. Some can be up to 100 feet (30 m) high. Skull Rock is the most famous. Erosion has caused it to look like a giant skull. The park has more than 8,000 climbing routes for all levels of rock climbers. Joshua Tree is also a destination for hiking, biking, and backpacking.

PARK ANIMALS

Many desert insects and animals rely on Joshua trees. Yucca moths lay their eggs in the trees' white flowers. More than 25 bird species use the trees for their nests. Seeds from Joshua trees are food for many small animals, including antelope squirrels, jackrabbits, and wood rats.

In higher elevations of the park, juniper and pinyon trees grow. These areas support many animals. Large mammals include coyotes and desert bighorn sheep.

Joshua trees and yucca plants rely on yucca moths for pollination.

KATMAI NATIONAL PARK
Location: Alaska   **Established:** 1980

Winter temperatures in Katmai National Park can reach −35 degrees Fahrenheit (−37°C), causing lakes and other water features to freeze.

Katmai National Park encompasses 5,741 square miles (14,870 sq km) in southern Alaska. It can only be reached by boat or plane. Novarupta, a volcano in the region, erupted in 1912. It was one of the biggest volcanic eruptions in world history. An ash cloud rose about 19 miles (32 km) into the air. The lava from the eruption came from magma underneath Mount Katmai, which was 6 miles (9.7 km) from Novarupta. As the magma drained, Mount Katmai collapsed. The eruption burned plants in nearby Ukak Valley to cinders. The heat caused steam to rise in the valley, giving it the nickname the Valley of Ten Thousand Smokes.

Katmai National Park is one of the most active volcanic regions in the world. There are at least 14 active volcanoes in the park. Scientists monitor volcanic activity in the park to prepare for major eruptions.

Mount Douglas is one of the active volcanoes in Katmai National Park. Its caldera is filled with water.

Harbor seals can be seen in Katmai National Park. They live in groups as protection against predators.

WILDLIFE

Katmai National Park includes coastlines, forests, tundra, and lakes. There are 42 mammal species, such as moose, caribou, lynx, and snowshoe hares, in the park. The coastline areas are home to sea lions, sea otters, porpoises, and seals. Beluga whales, gray whales, humpback whales, and orcas often pass through the waters of the park during their migrations.

Each summer, millions of sockeye salmon swim from the Bering Sea off Alaska's coast and return to a river in the park

to breed. This journey is called a salmon run. Salmon are an important food source for many animals, including grizzly bears. The bears are often seen catching fish along streams during the salmon run.

Grizzly bears wait upstream to catch sockeye salmon as the fish return to their breeding grounds.

KENAI FJORDS NATIONAL PARK
Location: Alaska   **Established:** 1980

Erosion formed the spires and cliffs of Resurrection Bay in Kenai Fjords National Park.

More than half of the 936 square miles (2,424 sq km) in Kenai Fjords National Park is covered in ice. A fjord is a narrow sea inlet between cliffs. Kenai Fjords is located on the Kenai Peninsula in southern Alaska. The park's backcountry has no trails or roads. Visitors use kayaks to explore remote areas like Bear Glacier Lagoon. It is a clear lake filled with icebergs.

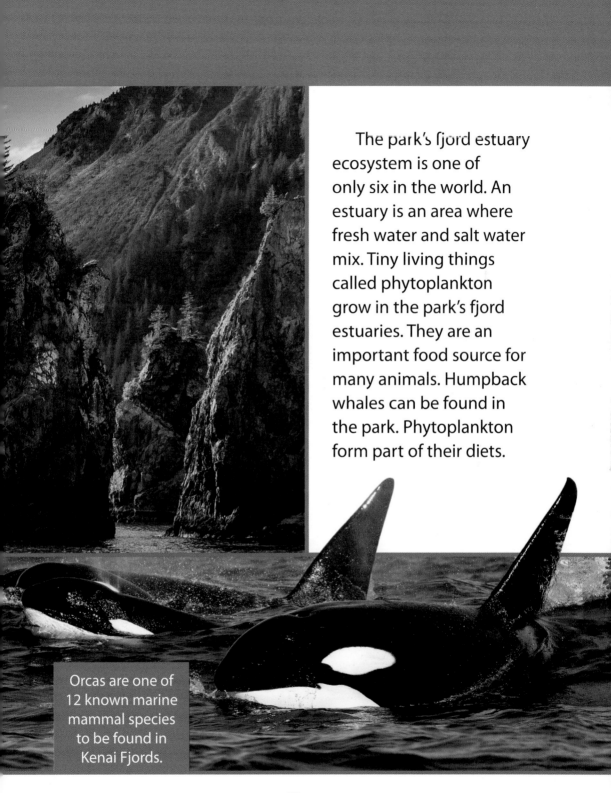

The park's fjord estuary ecosystem is one of only six in the world. An estuary is an area where fresh water and salt water mix. Tiny living things called phytoplankton grow in the park's fjord estuaries. They are an important food source for many animals. Humpback whales can be found in the park. Phytoplankton form part of their diets.

Orcas are one of 12 known marine mammal species to be found in Kenai Fjords.

GLACIERS

Kenai Fjords is known for the Harding Ice Field. This sheet of ice stretches for approximately 695 square miles (1,800 sq km). The ice in some parts of the ice field is more than 2,133 feet (650 m) thick.

The Harding Ice Field Trail is a challenging hike that takes about eight hours. It offers close-up views of the ice field and its glaciers.

The glaciers in Kenai Fjords formed during the Ice Age, approximately 25,000 years ago.

The glaciers in Kenai Fjords formed over millions of years. They began as snowfall. Cool summer temperatures kept the snow from melting. Over time, the snow compressed and became glaciers.

Exit Glacier is a famous glacier in Kenai Fjords. The glacier spreads across a mountain slope, dropping 3,000 feet (914 m) in just a few miles. Climate change has affected the glaciers in the park. Rising temperatures have caused Exit Glacier to shrink by more than 2,300 feet (701 m) since 2009.

KINGS CANYON NATIONAL PARK
Location: California   **Established:** 1940

The Kings River flows for 81 miles (130 km) in California. Kings Canyon National Park protects a section of this river.

Kings Canyon National Park is located in the Sierra Nevada, a mountain range in California. It covers 721 square miles (1,867 sq km). It is located next to Sequoia National Park. Kings Canyon also has some of the world's largest sequoia trees. Many are in Grant Grove, which covers just a small portion of the park. This is the home of the General Grant Tree, which is a popular tourist attraction. This sequoia tree is one of the largest in the world. It stands at 267 feet (81 m) tall and almost 29 feet (8.8 m) wide. It is between 1,800 and 2,000 years old. The tree was named after President Ulysses S. Grant.

The General Grant Tree is nicknamed the Nation's Christmas Tree.

California quail can be seen in the park near shrubs and rocks.

Kings Canyon is one of the deepest canyons in the United States. One section of the canyon plunges for 8,200 feet (2,499 m). Cedar Grove is the valley at the base of Kings Canyon. It includes Roaring River Falls, a waterfall that plunges through a narrow opening in the canyon's rock walls.

The North Dome and the Grand Sentinel are other major features of the park. These tall rock formations tower over Cedar Grove. Both have steep faces that attract advanced rock climbers.

THINGS TO DO

Visitors can take hiking trails to view the park's huge sequoia trees up close. Other trails lead to high observation points where people can enjoy views of the canyons and forests. The park also offers guided tours on horseback. During the winter, people visit the park to ski and snowshoe.

Kings Canyon has hundreds of miles of hiking trails.

Kobuk Valley National Park is one of the least visited national parks. The park is in a very remote area of northwestern Alaska. The only way to get to the park is by plane. It is located above the Arctic Circle and includes 2,734 square miles (7,082 sq km).

Kobuk Valley National Park includes three sand dunes, known as the Great Kobuk Sand Dunes. The largest one, Great Kobuk, sits along the bank of the Kobuk River. The dunes spread across 30 square miles (77 sq km) and can be up to 100 feet (30 m) tall. They are so large that they can be seen

Kobuk Valley National Park includes the Kobuk River, sand dunes, boreal forests, and mountains.

Caribou swim across the Kobuk River during their migration.

from space. The sand dunes were formed by glaciers more than 14,000 years ago. The Great Kobuk Sand Dunes are constantly moving. Although the park is in the Arctic, summer temperatures on the dunes can reach 100 degrees Fahrenheit (37.8°C). The dunes are home to the Kobuk locoweed, a plant that doesn't grow anywhere else in the world.

CARIBOU

Kobuk Valley National Park is famous for its caribou. Twice a year, the Western Arctic caribou herd travels through the park. The herd has about 188,000 individuals. It is the largest caribou herd in Alaska and one of the largest herds on Earth. The caribou migrate more than 140,000 square miles (362,600 sq km).

LAKE CLARK NATIONAL PARK
Location: Alaska   **Established:** 1980

Cook Inlet in Lake Clark National Park is home to brown bears and other wildlife.

Lake Clark National Park stretches for 6,297 square miles (16,309 sq km). It has a rich variety of ecosystems, including forests, lakes, volcanoes, and glaciers. It is located where the Alaskan and Aleutian mountain ranges come together. Lake Clark, for which the park is named, is 40 miles (64 km) long and is surrounded by mountains. The Chilikadrotna, Mulchatna, and Tlikakila Rivers flow through the park.

The park has two active volcanoes, Redoubt and Iliamna. Redoubt has erupted four times in the last 100 years, including a major ash explosion in 2009. Smoke can often be seen rising from Iliamna, but it has had fewer recent eruptions than Redoubt. As of 2022, Iliamna had not erupted since 1867.

WHY THE PARK WAS CREATED

Every year, more than 270,000 sockeye salmon return to Lake Clark to spawn, or breed. These fish are a keystone species for many ecosystems in the park. A keystone species is one that many other species depend on. Without this species, other plants and animals in the ecosystem would suffer. Lake Clark National Park was created partly to protect this important fish.

The park was also created to preserve resources for the Dena'ina people. The Dena'ina have lived in the Lake Clark region for thousands of years. Today, the Dena'ina live, hunt, and fish within park boundaries.

Fishing at Lake Clark National Park is most popular during the salmon run, which occurs from July through August.

LASSEN VOLCANIC NATIONAL PARK

Location: California **Established:** 1916

The summit of Lassen Peak reaches 10,461 feet (3,189 m), offering fantastic views of the surrounding parkland.

Lassen Volcanic National Park is located on 166 square miles (431 sq km) of land in northwestern California. Lassen Peak, an active volcano, is the park's most significant feature. It is the southernmost volcano in the Cascade mountain range, which stretches from California to British Columbia, Canada.

Lassen Peak had a series of eruptions between 1914 and 1917, with the most severe eruption occurring in 1915. A cloud of ash rose more than 30,000 feet (9,144 m) into the air. The eruption caused avalanches and mudflows that destroyed the landscape. The park was created a year later to preserve the area for scientific study. Scientists have been able to learn more about volcanic activity.

Visitors today can still see the effects of the 1915 eruption, including lava pinnacles, lava mountains, and steam vents. The park also has hydrothermal activity. Visitors can view active steam vents and bubbling mud pots in areas such as Boiling Springs Lake. Mud pots are hot springs filled with boiling mud.

THE DIXIE FIRE

In 2021, the Dixie Fire moved through northern California after a tree fell on electrical lines. It burned 114 square miles (295 sq km) of Lassen Volcanic National Park. Parts of the park remained closed to the public in 2022. Areas affected by fire are at a higher risk of being impacted by flash floods and habitat loss.

Steam rises over Bumpass Hell, an area of Lassen Volcanic National Park that is known for its hydrothermal features.

MAMMOTH CAVE NATIONAL PARK
Location: Kentucky **Established:** 1941

Mammoth Cave National Park covers 83 square miles (214 sq km) in rural Central Kentucky. It was created to protect Mammoth Cave, the longest known cave system on Earth. People have mapped more than 400 miles (643 km) of caves.

The caves were formed over millions of years as acidic water eroded the limestone rock. This process created many spectacular Mammoth Cave formations. The Frozen Niagara formation is made of flowstone, waterfall-like curtains of rock

Approximately 4,000 people visit Mammoth Cave National Park each day during peak tourist season.

Cave crickets live near cave entrances, including in the Mammoth Cave system. They help scientists learn about ecosystem health in the caves.

along cave walls. Cave popcorn is another cave formation. It looks like round clusters of popcorn. Helictites hang from the ceiling in thin, branch-like shapes.

The caves are home to about 160 species, including the Kentucky cave shrimp. This eyeless, transparent creature is found only in Mammoth Cave. Several endangered bat species, including the Indiana bat and the northern long-eared bat, live in the cave too.

PARK HISTORY

Early peoples used the caves for thousands of years. Some cave areas have ancient petroglyphs on the walls. Stashes of ancient torches have been found in the caves. In the 1800s, US settlers built a saltpeter mine in one of the caves. Saltpeter is an ingredient used in gunpowder. Today, visitors can still see the remains of this mine and the tools the miners used.

MESA VERDE NATIONAL PARK
Location: Colorado   **Established:**1906

Mesa Verde National Park was the first park in the National Park Service created for cultural protection.

Mesa Verde National Park is an archaeological park. It encompasses more than 81 square miles (210 sq km) on the Colorado Plateau in southwestern Colorado. The park protects about 5,000 ancient American Indian archaeological sites and millions of artifacts. It also includes the ruins of 600 cliff dwellings. Many of these dwellings are built into the cliffs of Mesa Verde.

The Basketmaker people were the earliest inhabitants on the mesas. They lived in small pit houses on top of the mesas.

Petroglyphs, such as those at Mesa Verde National Park, tell ancient stories that have been passed down through the generations. These petroglyphs were made by ancestors to the Pueblo peoples.

Around the 1200s, people began building pueblos in alcoves along the cliff walls. Some pueblos had only one room. Others had hundreds of rooms. The largest cliff dwelling in the park is Cliff Palace. It has 150 rooms and 23 ceremonial areas called kivas. Cliff Palace housed about 100 people.

Mesa Verde protects pit houses made by the Ancestral Pueblo.

All plateau whiptail lizards are female. They are able to reproduce without a mate.

The cliff dwellers farmed crops such as corn, beans, and squash. They hunted deer and gathered wild plants. A severe drought began in the late 1200s, making it difficult to grow food. By 1300, the pueblos were abandoned. In 1888, two cowboys found the ruins. The park was created in 1906 to protect the cliff dwellings.

PLANTS AND ANIMALS

The park has several wildlife habitats, such as scrublands, pine forests, and juniper forests. They support more than 300 animal species. Reptiles, including the prairie rattlesnake and plateau whiptail lizard, can be found at Mesa Verde. Some plants, such as the Mesa Verde stickseed, grow only in the park.

MOUNT RAINIER NATIONAL PARK

Location: Washington   **Established:** 1899

Wildflower blooms in Mount Rainier National Park tend to peak in mid-July to early August.

Rising 14,410 feet (4,392 m), Mount Rainier is the centerpiece of Mount Rainier National Park. The park covers 369 square miles (957 sq km). About 97 percent of the park is designated wilderness area.

Mount Rainier is the tallest volcano in the contiguous United States. It is an active volcano. Visitors can see steam vents and bubbling mineral springs in the park.

Mount Rainier has 25 main glaciers, and the largest is Emmons Glacier. It covers about 4.3 square miles (11 sq km). Carbon Glacier is the deepest glacier in the contiguous United States. The ice is nearly 700 feet (213 m) thick in some places. Nisqually Glacier is one of the most popular glaciers in the park. It is easily accessible, with a short hike to a viewing point.

The Skyline Trail offers close-up views of some of Mount Rainier's glaciers.

Climbers attempting to summit Mount Rainier stay at Camp Muir to adjust to the altitude.

Pikas can be found in boulder fields in Mount Rainier National Park.

PLANTS AND ANIMALS

There are three life zones in Mount Rainier National Park. Each is at a different elevation range. Some plants and animals live in only one zone. Others, such as bears, mountain lions, and coyotes, move between zones.

The forest zone covers more than half the park. It is found at 1,700 to 5,000 feet (518 to 1,524 m). Squirrels, beavers, and many bird species live in this zone. The subalpine zone is located at 5,000 to 7,000 feet (1,524 to 2,133 m). Hundreds of wildflower species grow in this zone. The park's glaciers are located in the alpine zone. This zone has an altitude of 7,000 to 14,410 feet (2,133 to 4,392 m). Mountain goats, marmots, and pikas can be seen in the alpine zone.

NATIONAL PARK OF AMERICAN SAMOA

Location: American Samoa   **Established:** 1988

The National Park of American Samoa is the only US national park in the southern hemisphere. It is located in American Samoa, a US island territory in the Pacific Ocean. The park includes sections of three volcanic islands: Taū, Ofu, and Tutuila. It covers 21 square miles (55 sq km) of land and ocean.

The National Park of American Samoa was also founded to preserve Samoan culture. People have lived on the Samoan Islands for approximately 3,000 years. The park protects the land and wildlife that have become part of the Samoan lifestyle. Some Samoan people live in villages within the park.

Only about 5,000 people visit the National Park of American Samoa each year.

Some fish species live amid sea anemones.

PLANTS AND ANIMALS

The park has mixed-species paleotropical rain forests. This means there are no dominant plant or animal species there. This rain forest is the only one of its kind in the National Park System. Small mammals such as mice, rats, and bats live in the rain forests. Three species of bats are native to the park. Reptiles such as geckos, skinks, and snakes are also found there.

The park supports more than 250 species of coral and more than 950 species of fish. Common fish include damselfish, wrasse, and parrotfish. Blacktip reef sharks and hawksbill sea turtles also swim through the waters. Many marine mammals, including humpback whales and dolphins, are also found in the park's waters.

NEW RIVER GORGE NATIONAL PARK
Location: West Virginia   **Established:** 2021

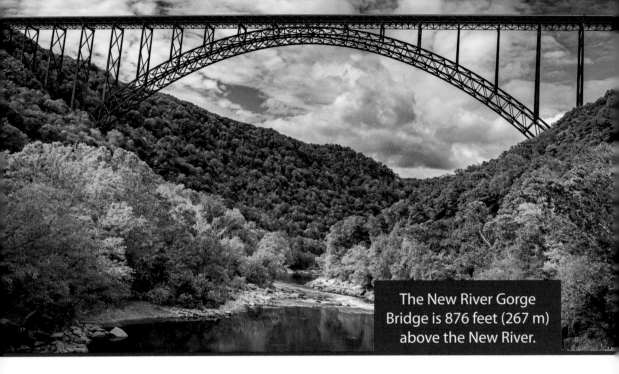

The New River Gorge Bridge is 876 feet (267 m) above the New River.

New River Gorge National Park includes 53 miles (85 km) of the New River and more than 109 square miles (283 sq km) of the gorge and surrounding forests. Reaching depths of 1,600 feet (487 m), New River Gorge is the deepest gorge in the Appalachian Mountains. Over millions of years, the river eroded the surrounding Nuttall sandstone to form deep canyon cliffs.

The New River Gorge bridge stretches 3,030 feet (924 m) over the gorge. It is the longest single-span arch bridge in the western hemisphere. It is the third-highest bridge in the United States and one of the most photographed areas in West Virginia. Grandview is an area of the park that offers overlook views of the river and gorge.

The park protects the Appalachian Flatrock Community. This rare habitat is a flat sandstone area near the river. Many plants that grow there are not found in other areas of the park. The park also protects endangered animals, such as the Allegheny wood rat, Indiana bat, and Virginia big-eared bat.

THINGS TO DO

New River Gorge has plenty of hiking trails through the forests. The park can also be explored by car by going on scenic drives along the rim of the canyon. Those who want to spend time on the water can enjoy fishing and white water rafting.

The southern portion of the New River has rapids more suitable for beginning white water rafters than the northern portion.

NORTH CASCADES NATIONAL PARK

Location: Washington   **Established:** 1968

North Cascades National Park sits on the North Cascade range, a chain of mountains that stretches more than 500 miles (805 km). This mountain range is nicknamed the American Alps for its majestic landscape. The park covers a total of 1,069 square miles (2,768 sq km). It includes the Ross Lake and Lake Chelan national recreation areas.

Diablo Lake in North Cascades National Park is known for its turquoise color.

People hiking in North Cascades National Park during the winter should be prepared for snow and cold temperatures.

The park gets an average of 633 inches (1,607 cm) of snowfall each year. The western region of the park receives more snow than the eastern part. With more than 300 glaciers, the park has the most glaciers of any national park in the contiguous United States. But most of the park's glaciers have shrunk due to climate change.

Douglas firs in the North Cascades can grow to be more than 250 feet (76 m) tall.

PLANTS AND ANIMALS

Groves of old-growth forests thrive in the park's backcountry. These forest areas are a mix of ancient trees and younger trees. One of the largest old-growth groves is along the Big Beaver Creek. The 200-foot (61 m) western cedar trees in this area are more than 1,000 years old. Other trees in the old-growth forests include Douglas firs and western hemlocks.

The park supports more than 75 mammal species. Some, such as the gray wolf, the Canada lynx, and the grizzly bear, are endangered or threatened. The fisher is a weasel-like mammal that once lived in the park. It is the only animal that hunts porcupines. Fishers were hunted to extinction in the area. Today, a program is working to reintroduce the animal to the park.

Fishers are able to climb trees but spend most of their time on the ground.

OLYMPIC NATIONAL PARK

Location: Washington   **Established:** 1938

Few animals and plants can survive at the peak of Mount Olympus due to the harsh climate.

Olympic National Park encompasses 1,442 square miles (3,735 sq km) in northwestern Washington. The park is named after its Mount Olympus, which rises 7,980 feet (2,432 m) above sea level. The park protects three different ecosystems: beaches, forests, and mountains. Together, they support a great diversity of plant and animal life.

Rocky structures called sea stacks can be seen at Second Beach in Olympic National Park.

The park's 73-mile (117-km) coast has rocky beaches and tide pools. The tide pools are home to many types of sea creatures. Barnacles cling to the rocks. Colorful sea stars and sea urchins can be seen in the tide pools. Shellfish can be found on the edge of the beaches. Along the coast, seabirds nest in the rocks. This habitat is also home to harbor seals, sea otters, and Steller sea lions.

Old-growth temperate rain forests grow in the park's valleys. Trees include the Sitka spruce, western hemlock, Douglas fir, and western red cedar. Many trees are several

The Hoh Rain Forest in Olympic National Park receives approximately 140 inches (356 cm) of precipitation each year.

hundred years old. Roosevelt elk, the largest elk species in North America, live in these forests.

More than 100 glaciers cover the park's mountain peaks. Blue Glacier is the largest glacier in the park. It is 900 feet (274 m) thick and 2.6 miles (4.2 km) long.

Sea stars cling to the tide pool rocks.

THINGS TO DO

Olympic National Park has hiking trails that allow visitors to explore all the park's ecosystems. North Coast and South Coast trails take hikers along the beaches. Northside trails wind through the mountains. Hikers on the southside trails enjoy walks through the forests.

Many people enjoy exploring the park's tide pools. Mora's Hole in the Wall is a popular destination. It can be explored only at low tide.

PETRIFIED FOREST NATIONAL PARK

Location: Arizona   **Established:** 1962

Petrified Forest National Park protects one of the largest collections of petrified wood in the world.

Petrified Forest National Park covers 346 square miles (896 sq km) of land. The park is known for its petrified logs. When something is petrified, it has turned into stone. Millions of years ago, the park was part of a pine forest and river. Some trees fell into the river. The wood filled with water and a mineral from volcanic ash called silica. These trees were buried in mud and sediment. Over time, the minerals in the wood turned into stone. The colorful quartz crystals in the logs have a rainbow hue. The Rainbow Forest has the largest and most colorful logs in the park.

The park also includes the Painted Desert, which stretches for 150 miles (241 km) to the Grand Canyon. The desert is named for its colorful stone formations, such as the Blue Mesa. The Blue Mesa has blue, gray, peach, purple, and white stripes on its sides.

HUMAN HISTORY

The park protects ancient American Indian ruins. Newspaper Rock has more than 650 petroglyphs that were made by the Ancestral Puebloans. Some of the petroglyphs may have been carved as long as 2,000 years ago. Puerco Pueblo is another park site with ties to the Ancestral Puebloans. Around 1300, this ancient village was home to approximately 200 people.

Many American Indian ancestors added petroglyphs to Newspaper Rock over hundreds of years.

PINNACLES NATIONAL PARK

Location: California   **Established:** 2013

Pinnacles National Park covers 41.6 square miles (108 sq km) in west central California. The park is divided into two sections, which are connected by hiking trails. Both areas include canyons, caves, enormous boulders, and pinnacles. These are the tall rock towers that the park is named after.

The pinnacles began to form approximately 23 million years ago. The park sits on top of a volcanic field. Magma from deep underground rose to the surface and hardened into rock. Over time, erosion and the movement of earth's crust shaped the rocks into the pinnacles seen today.

Before becoming a national park, the Pinnacles region was protected as a national monument as early as 1908.

As part of the condor recovery program, condors in Pinnacles National Park are tagged to help record information. Condors with tan tags hatched between 2018 and 2019.

The park is also known for its talus cave systems. Bear Gulch Cave and Balconies Cave are two examples. Talus caves form when falling rocks lodge against each other in a ravine or small canyon. Another notable park feature is Bear Gulch Reservoir. It is famous for its clear water and spectacular views of the surrounding gorge.

WILDLIFE

The park is home to many types of animals, including 14 species of bats. All of these bats eat insects. Some species drink nectar and pollinate flowers. Many park animals are threatened or endangered, including the California tiger salamander and the Sacramento perch. The Pinnacles shield-backed katydid, the big-eared kangaroo rat, and the Pinnacles riffle beetle are found only in the park. Critically endangered California condors also live in the park. Pinnacles is part of a condor recovery program.

REDWOOD NATIONAL PARK

Location: California   **Established:** 1968

Redwoods can grow to be 22 feet (6.7 m) thick at the base.

Redwood National Park preserves some of the last remaining redwood forests in the world. The park covers 206 square miles (534 sq km) along the northern California coast. It includes old-growth forests, prairies, grasslands, beaches, creeks, and rivers. Giant redwood trees can grow more than 350 feet (106 m) tall. That is taller than the Statue of Liberty. Redwoods can live for more than 500 years. These trees are the major attraction of the park, which has dozens of hiking trails to allow visitors to see the trees up close.

Redwood forests once stretched for millions of acres in Northern California. But logging companies began cutting down the trees in the 1850s. By the 1960s, more than 90 percent of the redwood forests had disappeared. The park was created in 1968 to protect the remaining forests. The park expanded to include three California state parks in 1994. Today, both national park and state park employees work in the park.

Redwood National Park has campgrounds that allow visitors to camp among the ancient trees.

WILDLIFE

The park protects several endangered species, including the Steller sea lion. Birds such as the marbled murrelet are threatened. Though this bird spends much of its time in the ocean, it breeds and nests in the forest.

Better known for its forests, Redwood National Park also has beaches.

Marbled murrelets are threatened due to habitat destruction and oil spills.

The park includes 40 miles (64 km) of rocky Pacific Ocean coastline. During low tide, tide pools are filled with sea stars, anemones, crabs, snails, and sea cucumbers. The beach attracts seabirds such as sandpipers, gulls, and brown pelicans. A pod of gray whales lives in the ocean off the park's coastline.

The Rocky Mountains stretch 3,000 miles (4,828 km) from New Mexico to British Columbia. Rocky Mountain National Park protects 415 square miles (1,075 sq km) of these mountains. The park is known for its sweeping scenery and snowcapped peaks. It is one of the most visited national parks, with more than four million visitors each year. Park elevations range from 7,860 to 14,259 feet (2,396 to 4,346 m). This includes 77 mountains that rise more than 12,000 feet (3,658 m). Twenty-four of these peaks are more than 13,000 feet (3,962 m) above sea level. Longs Peak is the tallest mountain in the park.

In addition to mountains, Rocky Mountain National Park includes forests, lakes, and meadows.

Mountain goats have wide hooves with two toes that help them climb mountains.

The park has three distinct life zones. The montane zone lies at the lowest elevation and has the most wildlife diversity. Above that, the subalpine ecosystem supports evergreen forests and many bird species. One-third of the park's land lies in the high-elevation alpine zone.

Some parts of Rocky Mountain National Park can be explored on horseback.

OUTDOOR ACTIVITIES

Rocky Mountain National Park has many kinds of outdoor activities. Visitors can camp at one of five campgrounds. More than 50 lakes are available for fishing. People enjoy photography and horseback riding too.

Hiking is another popular activity, and the park has many trails. About 30 miles (48 km)

of the Continental Divide National Scenic Trail run through the park. The Continental Divide is the line along the Rocky Mountains splitting North America into western and eastern parts. Other scenic trails at Rocky Mountain National Park lead to the park's beautiful mountain lakes. These bodies of water include Dream Lake, Emerald Lake, Jewel Lake, and Nymph Lake.

Parts of Rocky Mountain National Park get nearly 20 inches (51 cm) of snowfall each year, making the park a popular destination for cross-country skiing.

SAGUARO NATIONAL PARK

Location: Arizona   **Established:** 1994

Saguaro cacti are slow growing, growing about 1 inch (2.5 cm) every ten years. They produce their first flowers after approximately 70 years.

Saguaro National Park consists of two separate sections that total 143 square miles (370 sq km) of land in southeastern Arizona. The Rincon Mountain District lies east of the city of Tucson, and the Tucson Mountain District is to the west. The park was created to preserve the saguaro cactus and the Sonoran Desert ecosystem.

Saguaros can grow 50 feet (15 m) tall and live up to 250 years. They have a forked shape, with arms rising upward. They are found only in parts of the Sonoran Desert. The saguaro cactus flower is Arizona's state flower. The skin of a saguaro cactus has many ridges, or pleats. These allow the cactus to expand and contract to hold water.

WILDLIFE

Many animals depend on the saguaro for habitat and food. Birds such as the gilded flicker and Gila woodpecker make holes to build their nests inside the cactus. Other birds, including elf owls and purple martins, take over these nests when they become empty. Hawks and other birds may make nests in the cactus's arms. In the early summer, bats drink nectar from the saguaro flower and pollinate the cactus. The cactus fruit is also a food and water source.

In addition to the cacti, the park is also known for its water pools called tinajas. The park has hundreds of tinajas in the desert's bedrock. *Tinaja* is Spanish for "large earthen jar." These pools are vital water sources for animals.

Great horned owls may make their nests in the arms of saguaro cacti.

SEQUOIA NATIONAL PARK

Location: California   **Established:** 1890

Sequoias can grow to be 40 feet (12.2 m) thick at the base.

Sequoia National Park is nicknamed the Land of the Giants. The park protects giant sequoias, the largest trees in the world. The park covers 631 square miles (1,634 sq km). It is the second-oldest national park after Yellowstone. The park has the world's largest tree by volume, nicknamed the General Sherman Tree. It stands 275 feet (84 m) tall and is about 2,200 years old. It grows in a sequoia grove known as the Giant Forest.

Sequoia National Park was the first national park created to preserve a living species. From 1891 to 1913, the park was protected by Buffalo Soldiers, a group of Black soldiers. They served as park rangers, defending against poaching and illegal logging. Captain Charles Young was their leader. He became the first Black superintendent of a national park.

In 1940, Kings Canyon National Park was established next to Sequoia National Park. The National Park Service operates them together as Sequoia and Kings Canyon National Parks. The parks contain caves that support many species that do not live anywhere else, including unique spiders. Lilburn Cave, which lies in both parks, is the longest cave in California.

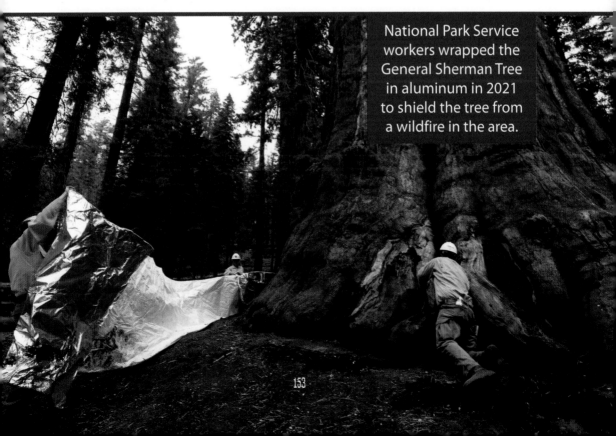

National Park Service workers wrapped the General Sherman Tree in aluminum in 2021 to shield the tree from a wildfire in the area.

The cave system connecting Sequoia and Kings Canyon contains more than 275 caves.

WILDLIFE

The park has several life zones with a diversity of species. The lowland foothills have rich forests where bears, skunks, gophers, and several reptile species live. Sequoias are found in the montane zone. Mountain lakes and wild meadows are found in the subalpine and alpine zone. Smaller mammals such as rabbits, pikas, and marmots live here. The endangered bighorn sheep is also found in this zone.

Marmots are the largest members of the squirrel family.

SHENANDOAH NATIONAL PARK

Location: Virginia   **Established:** 1935

Shenandoah National Park's rolling hills and wilderness cover 312 square miles (808 sq km) in central Virginia. The park is located in the Blue Ridge region of the Appalachian Mountains. Skyline Drive is the only road through the park. It winds for 105 miles (169 km), offering spectacular views of the landscape.

A short hike to the Stony Man viewpoint in Shenandoah National Park allows visitors to see the surrounding Shenandoah Valley.

Dark Hollow Falls is located near Mile 50.7 of Skyline Drive.

American Indian peoples, including members of the Cherokee nations, lived in the Shenandoah area for thousands of years. By the 1750s, European settlers had forced them from the land. In the 1800s, mining and lumber companies cut the forests and stripped the land. The park was created to restore the wilderness and preserve what was left. The government forced about 465 local families to move when the park was created in 1935. Hikers can visit Corbin Cabin, a historical landmark from that time. Skyland Resort was built in the late 1800s. Visitors today can still stay in rooms at the resort and enjoy the park.

The Skyland Resort offers horseback riding tours of the park.

Shenandoah is famous for its scenic mountain views along its more than 500 miles (805 km) of hiking trails. The hike to Old Rag Mountain is the most popular. Visitors are rewarded with amazing views of the lush, forest-covered hills below.

LIFE ON THE OUTCROPS

Shenandoah National Park is known for its rocky mountain outcrops. These places where rock emerges from the soil support endangered plant species, such as mountain sandwort and three-toothed cinquefoil. Some plants in the park are found nowhere else on Earth. Rare animals, such as the Shenandoah salamander, small-footed bat, and peregrine falcon, also live near the outcrops.

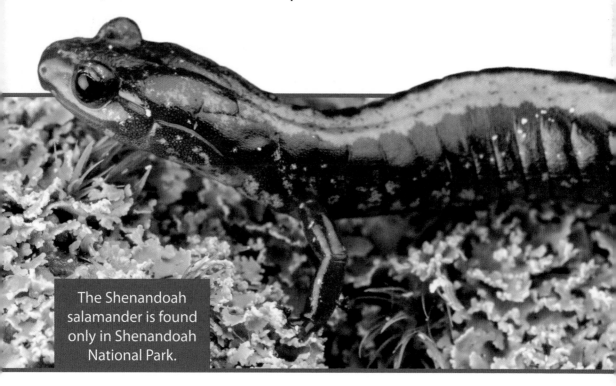

The Shenandoah salamander is found only in Shenandoah National Park.

Theodore Roosevelt National Park was created to honor the twenty-sixth president and his commitment to conservation. It is located in the Badlands of North Dakota. The park covers more than 110 square miles (285 sq km) along the Little Missouri River.

In 1883, Roosevelt came to the area to hunt bison. At that time, the habitats in the area were being damaged, and species were dying off. This affected him deeply. He became president in 1901 and was known for his conservation efforts. As president, Roosevelt created the US Forest Service,

The badlands in Theodore Roosevelt National Park contain hoodoos.

Pronghorn have large eyes and strong vision, allowing them to spot predators from far away.

150 national forests, and five national parks. By the end of Roosevelt's presidency, the US government added more than 36,000 square miles (93,100 sq km) of land under its protection.

HABITATS AND SPECIES

Today, most of the park consists of grassland prairie habitat. Native grasses like salt grass and western wheatgrass support grazing animals such as bison, elk, wild horses, bighorn sheep, pronghorn antelope, and deer. Prairie dogs also live in the grasslands. The park's river habitats sustain beavers and aquatic birds. Cottonwood forests in the floodplains are home to white-tailed deer and bird species such as golden eagles, turkeys, and owls. Coyotes, badgers, bobcats, and other predators can sometimes be seen in the park.

VIRGIN ISLANDS NATIONAL PARK
Location: US Virgin Islands   **Established:** 1956

Trunk Bay Beach is a popular beach in Virgin Islands National Park. It includes a snorkeling trail.

Virgin Islands National Park is a tropical place. The park encompasses 20 square miles (52 sq km) of land and ocean on the island of Saint John. This island is part of the US Virgin Islands, a US territory in the Caribbean Sea.

People have lived in the region for more than 3,000 years. Early cultures carved petroglyphs that can still be seen in Reef Bay. The Taíno people lived there in the 1400s. In 1493, the Italian explorer Christopher Columbus arrived. European countries colonized the region and fought over the land. By the 1700s, Saint John belonged to the Danes. They established sugarcane plantations. They also enslaved people from Africa and forced them to work on the plantations. Slavery was abolished in 1848. The plantations closed and fell into ruins. In 1917, the United States purchased Saint John, along with Saint Croix and Saint Thomas, from Denmark.

More than 20 hiking trails run throughout the park. Some lead to the ruins of sugar plantations. Visitors can learn about the island's history of slavery. People can also snorkel and view sea life near a reef in Hawksnest Bay.

LANDSCAPES AND ANIMALS

Virgin Islands National Park is known for its white sand beaches and lush tropical forests. Many people consider Trunk Bay Beach to be one of the world's most beautiful beaches. Today, the park supports more than 700 plant species.

The southern stingray is often found near the seafloor.

Sea turtles live in the seagrass habitats on Maho Bay Beach and Francis Bay Beach. The seagrass meadows also provide habitat for many fish and shellfish, including the queen conch. The park protects ocean habitats, such as coral reefs. These reefs are home to a wide variety of marine life, including angelfish, groupers, scorpion fish, lionfish, whale sharks, and stingrays.

VOYAGEURS NATIONAL PARK

Location: Minnesota   **Established:** 1975

Voyageurs National Park stretches for 341 square miles (882 sq km) in northern Minnesota. It contains Kabetogama Lake and parts of Sand Point Lake, Namakan Lake, and Rainy Lake. There are 26 smaller lakes and more than 500 islands within the park's borders. Much of the park can only be reached by water.

The waterways and rocky shores of Voyageurs National Park were formed by glaciers that melted about 11,000 years ago.

Pressure ridges may form in the park's lakes during the winter as the ice begins to melt.

The park was created to protect the area's wilderness. It also preserves the stories of the people who have lived there, from the ancient past to more recent times. American Indian peoples lived in the area as early as 10,000 years ago. By the 1600s, people of the Cree, Monsoni, and Ojibwe nations lived there.

In the late 1700s, voyageurs, or fur traders, used the waterways in the region to transport fur pelts. *Voyageur* is French for "traveler." The voyageurs used 25-foot (7.6 m) canoes made from birch, cedar, and spruce trees. The fur trade collapsed in the mid-1800s, in part because of changing fashions. Soon after, people used the area for mining, logging, and fishing.

LANDSCAPES AND ANIMALS

Voyageurs National Park includes forests, marshes, bogs, swamps, and lakes. These ecosystems support more than 50 mammal species and 100 bird species. Moose, beaver, bald eagles, and gray wolves live there. Fish such as walleye and northern pike swim in the lakes.

The northern lights occur throughout the year, but they are more visible during clear winter nights.

The ruffed grouse can be found in Voyageurs National Park. Males extend feathers on their necks as part of their mating rituals.

The park is known for its large rock outcrops. They are part of bedrock known as the Canadian Shield. This formation was created by prehistoric volcanic activity. The rocks are some of the oldest in North America.

WHITE SANDS NATIONAL PARK

Location: New Mexico   **Established:** 2019

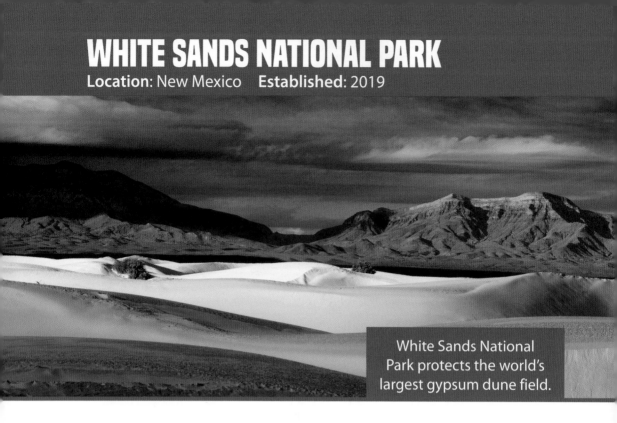

White Sands National Park protects the world's largest gypsum dune field.

White Sands National Park is located on 115 square miles (298 sq km) between the San Andres Mountains and the Sacramento Mountains in New Mexico. It protects almost half of the state's white sand dunes. The dunes cover more than 275 square miles (712 sq km) of desert in the Tularosa Basin.

The dunes were created about 10,000 years ago when Lake Otero dried up. Gypsum crystals formed as the water evaporated. Wind pushed the gypsum into dunes. When rain falls on nearby mountains made of gypsum, more gypsum washes down and settles in the basin.

During World War II (1939–1945), the White Sands area became a military testing area. The White Sands Missile Range was built. It was the location of the first atomic bomb test in 1945. The White Sands Missile Range includes the park and the surrounding area.

ANIMAL ADAPTATIONS

White Sands National Park supports more than 800 animal species. Some species have adapted to their white sand habitat. They are a light color to blend in with their surroundings. These include the Apache pocket mouse, the bleached earless lizard, and the sand-treader camel cricket. Several species of white moths also live in the park. These moths are native to the area and aren't found anywhere else in the world.

The bleached earless lizard blends in with its environment, allowing it to hide more easily from predators.

WIND CAVE NATIONAL PARK
Location: South Dakota   **Established:** 1903

Visitors to Wind Cave National Park often snap photos of the rock formations inside the cave system.

Wind Cave National Park covers 44 square miles (115 sq km) of caves and mixed-grass prairie. The Wind Cave system is more than 300 million years old. The cave complex has more than 149 miles (240 km) of caves, which include Petrified Clouds, Devil's Lookout, Pop Corn Alley, and Turtle Pass. The Wind Cave system is known for its unique boxwork formations. These are strips of minerals that form honeycomb shapes.

Wind Cave is important to several American Indian nations, including the Oglala Lakota. The Oglala Lakota call the cave *Oniya Oshoka* or *Maka Oniye*, meaning "the earth is breathing." It is part of their culture's story of people emerging from underground to live on the earth.

PROTECTED PRAIRIES

The park was established to protect not only the caves but also the mixed-grass prairie ecosystem. These prairies had once been home to bison, elk, and pronghorn. But these animals were overhunted. By the time the park was created, none were left in the area. The park successfully reintroduced these large mammals in 1913 and 1914. Today, the prairie habitat supports these animals and many others.

More than 100 bird species are found in the park. Among them are wild turkeys and sharp-tailed grouse, which gather in flocks on the grassy prairies. Park forests include maple, oak, willow, cottonwood, birch, pine, juniper, ash, and elm trees.

Bison are important to the prairie ecosystem. For example, they eat tall grasses, allowing animals such as prairie dogs to dig burrows in these areas.

Wrangell-Saint Elias National Park is America's largest national park. It covers 20,625 square miles (53,419 sq km) in the southeastern corner of Alaska. It is the world's largest protected wilderness. The park sits among four major mountain ranges: the Wrangell, Saint Elias, Chugach, and Alaskan. It holds nine of the sixteen highest mountain peaks in the United States. After Denali, Saint Elias is the second-highest peak in the United States. Wrangell-Saint Elias has only two roads. Most of the park can be reached only by plane.

Wrangell-Saint Elias National Park draws in avid adventurers who enjoy hiking and mountain climbing.

Saint Elias's peak is 18,008 feet (5,489 m) high.

More than one-third of the park is covered by enormous ice fields and glaciers. Bagley Ice Field is the world's largest ice field outside the Arctic Circle. It stretches for 127 miles (204 km). In some places, it is more than 3,000 feet (914 m) thick. Other giant glaciers are the Malaspina, Nabesna, and Hubbard.

The park includes the Kennecott Copper Mine and other mining sites. The Kennecott mine opened more than 100 years ago. The site was abandoned by 1938 after high-quality copper ran out. Kennecott is a ghost town and historical landmark. Chisana, Bremner, and Nabesna are former gold mining towns with abandoned structures that people can visit.

Approximately 200 to 300 people worked in the Kennecott Copper Mine. Another 300 people were in the nearby town. Today, the National Park Service is working to restore the town.

Dall sheep can weigh up to 300 pounds (136 kg).

WILDLIFE

The park's rich wildlife includes one of the largest Dall sheep herds in North America. More than 13,000 sheep live in the park's alpine regions. The park is also one of the only places where grizzly bears, black bears, and polar bears live together. Bison, caribou, coyotes, wolves, foxes, lynx, and wolverines live in the park too.

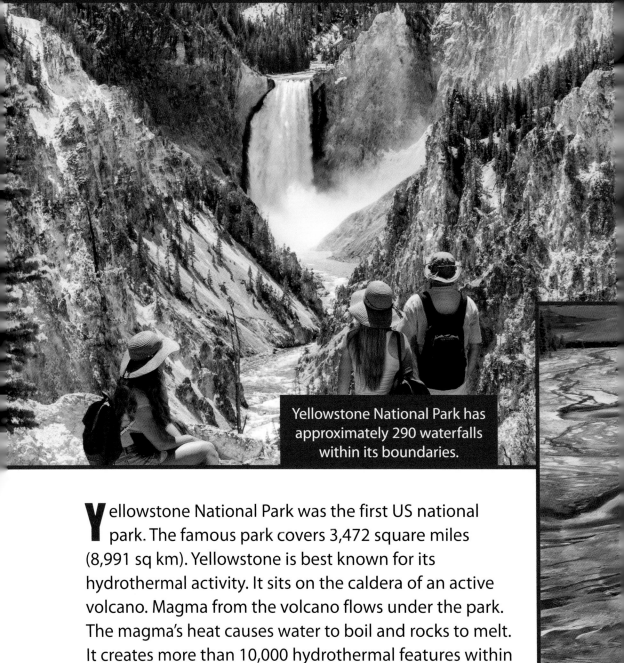

YELLOWSTONE NATIONAL PARK
Location: Idaho, Montana, and Wyoming   **Established:** 1872

Yellowstone National Park has approximately 290 waterfalls within its boundaries.

Yellowstone National Park was the first US national park. The famous park covers 3,472 square miles (8,991 sq km). Yellowstone is best known for its hydrothermal activity. It sits on the caldera of an active volcano. Magma from the volcano flows under the park. The magma's heat causes water to boil and rocks to melt. It creates more than 10,000 hydrothermal features within the park.

THINGS TO SEE

The Grand Prismatic Spring is a popular hydrothermal feature in the park. People can walk on a boardwalk next to the brilliantly colored hot spring. The spring has deep-blue water and is ringed in orange, yellow, and green. It is one of the largest springs in the world.

Mammoth Hot Springs showcases a lot of hydrothermal activity too. Hot water from deep underground bubbles to the surface. It mixes with the limestone in the area to create rocky terraces and mounds.

People can hike to an overlook to get a clear view of the Grand Prismatic Spring.

Typically it's difficult for park rangers to guess when a geyser will erupt. That's not the case with Old Faithful, which was named for its predictable eruption pattern.

The park has more than 500 active geysers, more than any other place in the world. A geyser is a hot spring that shoots columns of boiling water and steam into the air. Old Faithful is the park's most famous geyser. It erupts approximately every 90 minutes. The park's Steamboat Geyser is the tallest geyser in the world. It can shoot steaming water up to 400 feet (122 m) in the air.

In addition to its geysers, Yellowstone has beautiful scenery. The Grand Canyon of the Yellowstone River is 20 miles (32 km) long. The Upper Falls and Lower Falls plunge through the narrow canyon. Visitors also come to the park to watch wildlife such as bison, grizzly bears, and elk.

The Yellowstone River carved the Grand Canyon of the Yellowstone.

YOSEMITE NATIONAL PARK

Location: California **Established:** 1890

People are drawn to Yosemite for its valleys, waterfalls, meadows, and more.

Yosemite National Park covers 1,187 square miles (3,074 sq km) in the Sierra Nevada. It is one of the best-known national parks. President Abraham Lincoln signed the Yosemite Land Grant in 1864. This made Yosemite Valley and Mariposa Grove the first natural areas to be under federal protection.

The iconic Yosemite Valley is about 7 miles (11 km) long and less than 1 mile (1.6 km) wide. Famous rock formations, such as Half Dome and El Capitan, tower above the valley floor. El Capitan in Yosemite is a different formation than the peak of the same name in Guadalupe Mountains National Park.

Yosemite is known for its breathtaking waterfalls, including Yosemite Falls. This waterfall system is made of three separate waterfalls. Together, they tumble for 2,425 feet (739 m). Horsetail Fall is another famous waterfall in the park. It plunges from El Capitan. Sunsets during the winter cause the falls to look like they are on fire.

Mid to late February is the best time to see Horsetail Fall lit up by the sunset.

PLANTS AND ANIMALS

Yosemite has three giant sequoia groves. Mariposa Grove has more than 500 giant sequoias. It is the largest area of sequoias in the park. The Grizzly Giant sequoia in Mariposa Grove is 3,000 years old. Approximately 1,450 wildflower species bloom in the park, including monkey flowers, asters, and buttercups.

Yosemite is home to many animal species, including several threatened and endangered animals. The Sierra Nevada bighorn sheep and Sierra Nevada yellow-legged frog are both endangered. The fisher is another endangered animal. Fishers are related to weasels and live in forests. Their numbers have dropped due to hunting and habitat loss.

The Tunnel View gives visitors a sweeping look at Yosemite Valley.

Mariposa Grove has easy, moderate, and strenuous hiking trails that allow people to see the giant sequoia trees.

ZION NATIONAL PARK

Location: Utah   **Established:** 1919

Zion Canyon is one of the most popular tourist destinations in the US National Park System.

Zion National Park includes 229 square miles (593 sq km) in southeastern Utah. It protects sandstone canyons, cliffs, and waterways. Zion Canyon is the park's main feature. It is 15 miles (24 km) long and drops to depths of 3,000 feet (914 m). The Narrows is the narrowest part of the canyon. It is only 20 feet (6.1 m) wide in some spots. The Virgin River is the main river in the park and runs along the bottom of the canyon. It wore away the sandstone over millions of years, forming Zion Canyon.

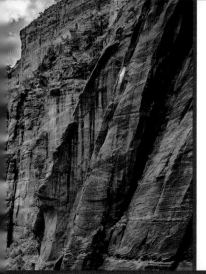

Along the river, cottonwood trees create a forest habitat. The forest supports deer, bobcats, foxes, squirrels, rabbits, and waterbirds. Higher in the canyons, juniper and pinyon forest habitats are homes to lizards and small mammals. At the highest elevations, elk and desert bighorn sheep live in ponderosa pine and Douglas fir forests.

The Watchman Trail is 3 miles (4.8 km) long and gives people a view of the Watchman Spire.

The Narrows has walls that are 1,000 feet (305 m) tall.

Kolob Arch is 287 feet (87 m) long.

THINGS TO SEE

Many people enjoy hiking through the Narrows during their visit to Zion. They wade through parts of the Virgin River at the bottom of the canyon. Some choose to begin the hike at the Temple of Sinawava. This rock formation marks the beginning of Zion Canyon. It has sheer cliffs and waterfalls.

Experienced hikers can tackle the Subway, a series of natural tunnels deep within the canyons. Hikers must climb down canyon walls. Parts of the trail overlap with North Creek at the bottom of the canyon.

The Kolob Canyons area is another scenic section of the park. People can hike through the canyons to Kolob Arch, one of the largest natural arches on Earth. The arch is made of sandstone.

GLOSSARY

archaeological
Relating to prehistoric cultures and their artifacts, monuments, and other remains.

astronomy
The study of outer space.

conservation
The planned protection and preservation of something.

contiguous
Touching or next to each other.

designated wilderness area
An official classification given by the US government to protect landscapes.

ecosystem
A community of organisms and their environment.

erosion
The process of wind, water, or ice wearing away rocks or the landscape.

geological
Relating to the science of Earth's history.

glacier
A large body of ice that slowly moves downhill.

habitat
A place where a plant or animal naturally grows or lives.

hydrothermal
Relating to hot water, especially underground.

mesa
A table-like rock formation.

migrate
To move from one area to another.

paleontologist
A scientist who uses fossils to study the distant past.

petroglyph
A rock carving.

pictograph
A rock painting.

TO LEARN MORE

FURTHER READINGS

McHugh, Erin. *National Parks: A Kid's Guide to America's Parks, Monuments, and Landmarks*. Black Dog & Leventhal, 2019.

Nickum, Mary Jo. *The Making of the Grand Canyon*. Aquitaine, 2020.

Ward, Alexa. *America's National Parks*. Lonely Planet, 2019.

ONLINE RESOURCES

Booklinks
NONFICTION NETWORK
FREE! ONLINE NONFICTION RESOURCES

To learn more about US national parks, please visit **abdobooklinks.com** or scan this QR code. These links are routinely monitored and updated to provide the most current information available.

INDEX

PHOTO CREDITS

ABDOBOOKS.COM

Published by Abdo Reference, a division of ABDO, PO Box 398166, Minneapolis, Minnesota 55439. Copyright © 2023 by Abdo Consulting Group, Inc. International copyrights reserved in all countries. No part of this book may be reproduced in any form without written permission from the publisher. Encyclopedias™ is a trademark and logo of Abdo Reference.

Printed in the United States of America, North Mankato, Minnesota.
102022
012023

THIS BOOK CONTAINS
RECYCLED MATERIALS

Editor: Angela Lim
Series Designer: Colleen McLaren

LIBRARY OF CONGRESS CONTROL NUMBER: 2022940664

PUBLISHER'S CATALOGING-IN-PUBLICATION DATA
Names: Lassieur, Allison, author.
Title: The national parks encyclopedia / by Allison Lassieur
Description: Minneapolis, Minnesota: Abdo Publishing, 2023 | Series: United States encyclopedias | Includes online resources and index.
Identifiers: ISBN 9781098290474 (lib. bdg.) | ISBN 9781098275792 (ebook)
Subjects: LCSH: National parks and reserves--Juvenile literature. | Parks--Juvenile literature. | United States--Juvenile literature. | Encyclopedias and dictionaries--Juvenile literature.
Classification: DDC 917.3--dc23